Autumn

Fires

By

M J Rutter

Acknowledgements

Who would have thought that a Dorset set summer romance would turn into a whole series following the lives of this special couple. I am so happy to have come this far on the journey and eager for it to continue.

My thanks, as always, goes out to my amazing family and friends, without your support and encouragement, I know I would never have come this far.

I have to be honest, I have written a lot of these and I feel I am always repeating myself. But I can't thank you all enough. To my husband and children, as always, I am so lucky to have you all on this journey with me.

My amazing Beta Team, Heidi Christiansen-Wynne, Susan Scott and Denise Roberts, there are no words to equate to my undying gratitude of you lovely ladies. You truly are a blessing and I am so lucky to have you on my team.

My awesome proof reader Becca Ponder, thank you so much, once again you have shone through.

A special thank you to my amazing cover designers, who have taken the Seasons Series on board and bought Kelsey and Jeremy to life with the beautiful covers you have created for me. You have given them a face and I can't thank you enough for all of the promoting and support you have given me, Rebecca and Angel, you truly are stars, keep shining.

A final thank you to you, my readers, I have said it a thousand times, without you, there is no point to writing. Your messages and reviews make it all worth it.

I'll keep writing as long as you keep reading.

Prologue

Sat here watching my son breathe is the single most satisfying thing in the world to me. He has a cold though and to most children the snuffle is nothing, runny nose, a little cough, yep, no problem, just dose him up with cough linctus and smother him with vapour rub. I wish it was that simple.

Harrison had just turned eight months old when he developed breathing problems, Jeremy and I rushed him to the hospital and they ran some tests. Our baby boy, our beautiful baby boy was diagnosed with the same congenital heart defect that killed my little brother, Ben. How could life be so cruel? He was transferred to Southampton and we have been travelling back and forth to there ever since.

With Harrison's second birthday approaching fast, his imminent operation follows just two months later, I am not sure if Jeremy and I are strong enough to cope. We broke before, will this break us too?

One

Kelsey

"I hate leaving him for the night," I grumbled and looked out of the window.

Jeremy sighed loudly, "Is that because you will miss him or because you don't trust me to look after *our* son properly?"

"Of course I trust you," I retorted, but did I? What if he forgot to give him his inhaler or medicine? What if Harrison needed me? What then?

"It's your best friend's birthday, you are going to sodding Poole for a pub crawl, not Majorca." Jeremy spat back bitterly.

He was tired, Harrison had had us both up the night before, he was only two and he had us wrapped around his little finger. My mum said I allow him too much attention and now he feeds from it. She would know more than anyone, she nursed my little brother Ben until his last breath. I shook my head, thinking about Harrison dying was unimaginable and caused pain to shoot through my heart.

He stopped the car on the quay to where Jude, Nicki, Shawna and Lou stood waiting for me. As they saw the car stop, they rushed forward, Jude opened the back door and cooed at Harrison. He lapped it up, four girls swooning over him, he was his father's son all right.

"Hi, Jez," Jude grinned.

"Hey," he sighed. She pulled a face at me. "He'll be fine," he told me. I nodded and leaned towards him to give him a kiss, he turned his face and allowed me to peck his cheek. Arse!

"Call me, if you need anything," I said as I unclipped my seatbelt.

"Just go, Kelsey, he will be okay with me, I am not stupid." He added sourly.

"I never implied that you were." I snapped and climbed out of the car.

"Mumma," Harrison cried.

"Be good for Daddy, okay?" I told him as he began to cry. I had hardly left him since he was diagnosed, I took a career break instead of returning to work, Jeremy was none too pleased about that too. "I'll see you in the morning."

"Yeah, have fun." He told me without looking at me. I closed the door and watched them drive off.

"Is everything okay?" Nicki asked.

I wanted to tell them that all we do is fight and argue, that we are so tired we hadn't had sex in three months, that nothing I say is right and everything I do is wrong, but I lied, "Sure, he's just tired."

"Once the operation is out of the way, you'll be back to normal in no time," she assured. I just wished I could believe her.

"Come on, girls," Jude announced, "Let's get the party going."

Nicki linked her arm with mine and we walked towards the Jolly Roger.

Outside, hordes of revellers sat drinking, laughing and joking, they were having a great time, I only wished I could say the same about me. I sat inside with the girls and smiled as they talked about work and Jude about her love life with Seb, Jeremy's cousin. They implied that they were tying the knot, but his parents put a stop to it, so had decided to just run away and get married at Gretna Green instead. I envied them, their lives all seemed so simple, why couldn't I have it easy for a change, why was my life such an up-hill battle?

I sipped at my vodka and coke and wondered if Harrison was okay. I knew Jeremy would be alright looking after him, he was a great father, but Harrison wasn't just any child, he was my world and the thought that he was sick and there was nothing I could to help, made me feel a failure. God knows, I sucked at being a wife.

We'd hardly had it easy and I lay there night after night beside him as he sleeps, I wonder if we should just have stayed apart. It had been sixteen months since Harrison was diagnosed and sixteen months since I actually felt like I had a husband. He showed me no affection or comfort and I know I was just as bad, but wasn't the job of a husband to be there when his wife fell?

Nicki noticed my apathy and bought over another drink. "Jude is worried about you," she told me as she sat down.

"I am worried about me," I grumbled lifting the glass and knocking it back. "He is going to leave me, Nicki, he will. He can't handle this and I think he blames me for Harrison's condition, after all, it came from my bloodline, not his."

"There is no way he would blame you." She disagreed. "He feels useless, incapable of protecting you and Harrison from this. He feels he has failed you." I looked at her and frowned. "He called Felix last week, Felix met him for lunch and they talked."

I heaved in a disgruntled breath, "So, he's talking behind my back, going out for lunch and I am at home living this nightmare day in and day out."

"That's not very fair, Kelsey, he is living it too." She snapped. My eyes filled with tears, I was being so selfish, of course he was living it too. "Sorry, I didn't mean to…"

"Yes you did," I sniffed and drained the glass. "I won't let this beat me." I stood from my seat, "Fancy another?"

"Sure," she smiled and I headed for the bar.

Have you ever tried getting drunk and no matter how many shots you have or how much you mix them, you stay as sober as a judge? Yep, that was me, I just couldn't seem to relax and enjoy Jude's night out. I worried constantly about Harrison and if Jeremy was coping okay. By ten o'clock I had tortured myself enough and told Jude I was getting a taxi to go home.

"You shouldn't have bloody bothered coming," she barked.

"Oh, I'm sorry, but my child has the same illness that killed my little brother," I retorted, "If anyone would understand I thought it would be you, but you are so wrapped up in the world of Jude…"

"If that's how you feel then go, but don't think I am ever going to be at the end of the phone when it all goes tits up for you again, because the way you are at the moment, we are all sick to the back teeth of it and I know Jez is pissed off with it too. You are destroying your marriage, but then, I wouldn't expect anything else from you, everything you touch turns to shit…" My eyes filled with tears, she was right, I was losing everyone because of my love for my child, but hearing her tell me something I already knew, confirmed it all the more. "Kelse, I am so…"

"Right," I cried and looked at them all staring at me. "I'm sorry, I'll just um, bye," I sniffed and hurried out into the night air.

"Kelsey," Nicki chased after me, "Kelsey, wait." I didn't stop and ran to the first taxi I could find, I climbed in and headed home.

When I got home to our house in Branksome, the living room light was on. I locked the front door and kicked off my shoes, while removing my jacket, I crept through the hall to the living room. Jeremy was asleep on the sofa with a file from work draped over his chest. I knelt on the floor in front of him and stared at his wedding ring, hanging loosely on his finger, he was losing weight again and I expected it was down to stress. His glasses were hanging off his face and as I slowly pulled them off, he snapped his eyes open.

"Kelsey," he frowned as he slowly sat up, "what are you doing home?"

"Well," I smiled, "I am drunk and extremely horny, and you know how horny I get when I drink way too much vodka." I leaned towards him and kissed him. He pulled back and frowned.

"You've been crying," he said sweeping my hair away from my eyes.

"I had a fight with Jude, she is such a bitch," I admitted and sat back on my heels. "She didn't want me to leave and all I wanted was to come home."

"Because of Harry?"

I frowned, I didn't like him calling him Harry, that wasn't his name, "Harrison," I corrected. "Not just because of him, I couldn't bear the thought of waking up in a hotel without you there." I said coyly.

He smiled warmly, we'd been living separate lives for months, I could see that now, see it etched on his unshaven, weary looking face. But he was still as gorgeous as ever and he was still mine, for that moment anyway. He dipped his head and pressed his lips to my shoulder, inhaling as he kissed me, I melted right there on the spot, my legs wouldn't move and my body warmed.

"So…" he said and kissed my shoulder again, "are we having an early night?"

"Yes," I smiled and took his hands in mine.

"I like you drunk," he grinned as excitement flashed in his amazing eyes.

"Funny, I like you too when I am drunk," I giggled taking his hand and leading him up the stairs.

As I stepped into our room Jeremy spun me around and lifted my dress over my head. Pushing the straps of my bra over my shoulders, he pressed against me from behind as he kissed my shoulders and neck, just the way I liked it.

We needed this, I needed him. I felt like a sun drenched flower that needed water and he was my water. I just hoped and prayed that we were too far lost to find our way back to each other. I turned to face him and began unbuckling his belt, I pulled his jeans down his legs and as I came back up his body, I lightly scratched my nails through the hairs on his legs. It caused goose bumps to rage his skin and he moaned softly. His huge erection pressed against his shorts and as he pulled his shirt over his head, I caught a whiff of his mouth watering aftershave that used to drive me wild.

I'd been so wrapped up in my world, I hadn't noticed that he had put some on, even though he hadn't shaved, I didn't care. I kissed his body as he fumbled with my bra clasp, suddenly it sprung open and my new bigger boobs fell free. Mouth to mouth we climbed onto the bed, I rested against the cool sheet as he pushed off his boxers, then gently moved his lips over my legs all the way up to my bellybutton.

Using one hand he pushed my underwear down to my ankles and smiled as I kicked them off to the floor, by this point I was melting, literally. No time for foreplay, I felt if he had touched me, I would have exploded. I pulled him to my lips,

"If we don't slow down, it will be over in seconds." He husked.

"If you don't hurry up, I will combust. I don't care, Jeremy, just make love to me, now." He smiled again and climbed between my legs, just before entering he stopped.

"In case I forget later, I love you, Mrs Buxton."

His worlds soothed my aching soul, it seemed months since I had heard that, "That sort of pillow talk will get you everywhere." I grinned and pulled him towards me.

The moment we connected all of my concerns seemed to float away. He was right, it didn't take long for either of us and I didn't mind, because we had those moments together and we so needed them. I loved him so much and would be heart-broken if I lost him, above everything else he was the other half of me and I knew we could never lose each other again.

I snuggled into his warm body, our pulses still racing and hearts slowing down, he stroked my arm with his thumb and it tickled slightly,

"Are you alright?" he asked.

"No," I frowned. "I have been a terrible wife to you, I have pushed you away and I don't deserve you. But if you forgive me, I promise to be a better wife."

"Sweetheart, where did this come from?" he asked.

"Tonight I realized how close I was to losing you. I can't lose you, Jeremy, you are my everything," I admitted.

"We're just a bit stressed and tired, love. I am not going anywhere."

"Well, that's good then, because neither am I." I squeezed his body tighter, fighting the tears in my eyes. "Can I ask you something?"

"Yes."

"Do you blame me for Harrison being sick?"

"What?" He sat up slightly. "Why would I?"

"Ben, my brother," I frowned.

"Kelsey, I would never blame you, Harry-sorry-Harrison is sick and he will get better after his op, it is just one of those things, you heard what the doctors said. Times have changed and he will pull through this."

"I hope so," I sighed sadly, he placed his hand under my chin and lifted my head.

"Sweetheart, he is a Buxton and we are stubborn, you should know that more than anyone. You are a good mother and wife, so we've drifted apart briefly, this is what we both needed and well, I hope you are not too tired, because…" he climbed on top of me, "I am ready to go again." He grinned.

There he was, eyes wild and sparkling, sensational smile and that little spark of arrogance, my Jeremy, my gorgeous, stubborn, cocky husband. Maybe I was just being over sensitive, I certainly felt so much better. It didn't take him long to get my mind off it all, in fact, nothing but feeling him inside of me could intrude on my mind at all.

Two

Jeremy

The second I turned my face away from her kiss I regretted it. Why was I being such a dick? Of course she was scared of leaving Harry; she hadn't left him since he was born, so this was a huge step for her. Instead of reassuring her, I acted out of spite and made her feel worse.

He cried all the way home and to be honest, I almost called her mobile. I could do this though, I had to prove to her I was capable and as soon as I lifted him out of his car seat he was fine, he needed a nappy change, but was fine. She was meant to have potty trained him over the summer, but that hadn't happened yet. I worked all day so felt I didn't have an opinion on the matter, after all it was Kelsey who was there with him all day every day.

I changed his nappy, put clean pyjamas on him and carried him into his cot-bed. I had a few contract papers to correct, so needed him to settle quickly. To my surprise he did, I kissed him goodnight and told him I loved him, feeling a pinch of guilt as I turned off the light. I had no right to speak to her like that, leaving him for the night was going to be hard, but we both needed it.

I missed what we had, although getting married while she was pregnant didn't give us much time for anything. Harry arrived and everything changed the day they told her about his heart. I felt I was losing her, she was becoming so wrapped up in that baby and it was as if I didn't matter anymore, that she no longer needed me and it left me feeling lonely and left out. Not to mention useless and incompetent.

I hoped this night away would not only give her a much needed break, but also the notion that he wasn't as delicate as she thought, that we could in fact enjoy the odd night out now and again.

I put on the TV, turning down the volume and sat with a glass of milk while reading over the contracts. I could have used a beer, but the last thing I wanted was for her to discover that I was that irresponsible prick she thought I was and drank while babysitting.

I loved my job at The Press in Blandford Forum, I got the job just after Kelsey and I got together, and I was keen to climb that ladder, so it meant the hours were long and sometimes I had to work at home. Discovering I needed glasses put a dent in my ego. My God, twenty-eight and needing glasses, that was bad by my standards. I thought I had a couple more years of youth left.

I worked through the contracts and by nine thirty I was so tired, I could hardly keep my eyes open. I swung my legs up onto the couch and tried so hard to fight my heavy eyelids, it was a battle I couldn't win, I remember hearing the news start and then I was floating.

My eyes snapped open making her jump, she smiled slightly and gazed into my eyes. I wasn't surprised to see her back at all, eyes twinkling and cheeks red with a healthy flush, she looked sensational, no doubt about it. I could never be angry at her for too long and when she offered me the one thing that had truly been lacking recently, I jumped at the chance.

I wanted her and I needed her as much as she needed me. As I eased inside of her, feeling her warmth surround me, I thought nothing would ever cause me to doubt my feelings again. We had found our way back again, we always did. Jez and Kelse, inseparable.

Harry screaming woke us both with a start, I could hear him choking, pushed off the covers and ran to his room. I lifted him from his bed, he felt hot and his breathing was raspy and laboured.

"Not again," I groaned and pressed my lips to the side of his head.

"What's wrong?" Kelsey asked wrapping her robe around her naked body.

"I don't know, I think he has that chest infection back. We need to get him to the hospital." I explained.

"Bloody hell," she said racing towards me, because she knew as well as I did, he would be there for weeks again if it was the same infection, it could lead to pneumonia and that would kill him. She took him from me and he rested his head against her shoulder.

"I'll get dressed." I told her and left the room.

Why our child, why was he so sick? It didn't seem fair, Harrison had already spent a huge part of his young life in Poole children's ward and if not there, he would be at Southampton. I feared this was where we were heading again.

I pulled my jeans on over my boxers, slipped my sockless feet into my trainers and grabbed my hoody off the back of the chair. I hurried back to her, she was humming to him while rubbing his back. His skin looked red and blotchy and I could see he wasn't at all well. I could also see her mind racing, her face full of guilt and regret, it didn't take long before she was back to being the stressed out, hot head who took her anger out on me.

"Give him to me," I said holding my hands out to her. "You need to get dressed."

"You said he would be alright," she snarled, "you said you could look after him and look, he is sick again and where are we going? To the sodding hospital," Harry started crying.

"Kelsey, go and get dressed," I groaned.

"Fine," she snapped and handed Harry to me as she passed me, "I'll never forgive you, Jeremy Buxton, for making me go out when I knew he was coming down with something."

"Oh," I yelled after jigging Harry up and down to calm him. "I am so sorry for thinking that you might actually need a bloody break."

I waited on the landing until she emerged wearing black leggings and a light pink hoody. She slipped her feet into her black Uggs and took Harry from my arms.

"I'll go and start the car," I huffed and ran down the stairs slamming the door behind me.

Harry cried all the way to the hospital. We never shared a word. She sat in the back trying to soothe him, but the more he cried, the more he coughed. When we arrived we headed up to the children's ward, pressed the buzzer and waited. As Janine, one of Harry's nurses approached the door, Kelsey finally spoke to me.

"You had better go and park the car," she said bluntly and without looking at me.

"Its fine where it is," I replied.

"I wasn't asking you," she frowned.

"Fine," I barked and walked away.

She was back, my ice queen, I loved her, but God knows at that moment, I loathed her too. I couldn't live like this anymore. I didn't want to admit we had failed, we'd had so much stacked against us, but to go from making love, to feeling like the lowest piece of shit ever not a few hours later, that crushed me.

I parked the car and ran across to the petrol station for a can of coke and some chewing gum, anything to delay my imminent return to her. I did have to go back to her though, I wanted to check on my son and I don't know why, but I thought she might actually need me, once she had calmed down.

I pressed the buzzer to the ward and waited for them to let me in. We had become so friendly with the nurses, Harry had spent a lot of his life with them, more them than us in all honesty. The door opened and the short, blonde haired nurse known as Tasha smiled,

"Hello, Jez," she grinned.

"Hey, Tasha, how are you?"

"Can't complain," she said. "Harrison is in room two."

"How is he?" I asked.

"He has a high temperature and a fever rash, Dr Muir will be here soon, he's been paged."

"Thanks," I sighed.

"To be honest, I don't think it's anything to do with his chest, but I am no doctor." She shrugged.

"Okay," I nodded and headed to the room hoping she was right. Harry was stripped to his nappy and lay in a cot. They had him wired up to a heart monitor and Janine gave a warm smile as I approached gingerly.

"He's okay," she assured with her Scot's accent.

"Thanks," I nodded.

"Dr Muir is on his way, this is just as a precaution," she explained.

"Yeah, Tasha said," I looked at Kelsey. She had been crying and my first instinct was to comfort her, but I always seemed to be the one to comfort her, who would comfort me?

We sat and waited for the doctor to arrive. I watched the sun rise over Poole Park lake and as planes streaked the early morning sky with jet fumes, I wondered how much more of this I could take.

"Ah, Mr and Mrs Buxton," Dr Muir announced as he strode into the room. He was as tall as me with dark grey hair and light blue eyes. He always looked tanned too, lucky bugger probably had a villa in the south of France or something, it was good to see him and he soon put our minds at ease.

"Hello, Dr Muir," Kelsey spoke her first words since I had returned from parking the car.

"So, let's have a look at you, young man," he said to Harry, who seemed a little better to me, but I daren't open my mouth. He pressed his stethoscope to Harry's chest and listened. "Well it's not a chest infection, in fact, his chest is very clear, judging by his rash I'd say it's a teething rash and he may have coughed up a little mucus, but other than that, he is fine. A little Calpol and plenty of fluids and he'll be as right as rain."

"Are you sure?" Kelsey checked.

"Positive, go home and get some rest. He is a tough, little cookie." He smiled. "Tougher than you think."

"Thanks," I smiled slightly.

"Sorry we wasted your time," Kelsey grumbled.

"You didn't, I told you I would come and see him anytime, Mrs Buxton, you were right to bring him in, this is why we are here. Better safe than sorry."

"Okay," she muttered and flashed her eyes at me, "thank you."

"Anytime," he smiled and signed Harrison's paperwork before leaving the room.

I stared after him for a long time after he left the room and then I turned back to the window while Janine and Tasha removed the wires from Harry. They fed him some breakfast before we were able to leave and as Kelsey carried him out, I walked on ahead to get the car from the car park.

Twelve quid later, I almost choked when I saw the cost of the ticket on the machine, I snatched the ticket out after paying and drove up the hospital ramp to collect them. At least it was Sunday and I could get some sleep, I was knackered, but I would not allow her to know this, I didn't want sympathy or anything from her. She had shouted at me again and it clearly wasn't my fault. Harry, like most kids his age, was teething. Maybe I over reacted too, still, it couldn't hurt for her to apologise.

We arrived home just after nine. She still hadn't said anything, though her face had softened, I could see she was pondering on the idea of admitting she was wrong, but she rarely did and I was not going to hold my breath.

As soon as we got inside the house, I locked the front door and headed up to our room. I kicked off my shoes and jeans and pulled my hoody back over my head. I climbed into bed and closed my eyes. I just wanted to go back a few hours to where I held my wife in my arms after making her moan my name into my ear as she orgasmed. I missed that, it had been months and in a split moment, it was gone again.

I felt someone sit beside me, my eyes opened and the room was only lit by the sun piercing through the crack in the curtains. Kelsey frowned,

"I uh, I made some chili, if you are um, if you are hungry."

"Thanks," I said and sat up.

"It's ready, so…" she stood.

"I'll take a quick shower and I'll be down," I promised. She walk towards the door and turned around.

"About last night, I am sorry, okay? I was wrong to blame you and…"

"I'm used to it," I said standing from the bed.

"What?"

"I said I am used to it. Every time Harry-uh-son, is sick, you take it out on me. I guess it comes with the job."

"Our marriage is not job," she frowned pursing her lips.

"Is that right? So why is it then that I have never had to work so hard at anything before in my life?"

"If that's how you feel," she grumbled.

"Yes, it is." I spat and left her standing in the bedroom.

We didn't speak for the rest of the day, she had pissed me off and now she knew she had. She went to bed early and I stayed up to watch a movie, I had slept too long to go to bed too early and when I did all I could do was lay there and listen to her breathe in the darkness. I had never felt so lonely while sharing a bed with someone before, it was crippling and I was actually relieved when my alarm went off at six.

My cousin, Sebastian, had started at the office on his return from Australia. Initially he and his girlfriend Jude had left for six months just after our wedding, that was shortened to three and then down to one month. They'd had one month in Oz and when he got back he started the job I had secured for him. It made sense and it meant that I got to see him more. He had been there for just over two years and I liked having him around if nothing else but for someone to talk to.

I parked my white Evoque in the usual spot under the willow tree and beeped on the alarm as I crossed the car park. I could see Seb getting out of his BMW and waved.

"Your wife has royally pissed my misses off," Seb announced as I approached him.

"My wife seems to piss everyone off lately," I retorted. "I'm sorry she messed Jude's birthday up, is she really upset?"

"You know Jude, called her all the selfish cows and bitches under the sun, she loves her really though."

"Glad someone does," I scoffed.

"What's this, more trouble in paradise?" he asked.

I nodded, "Yep, Harry was rushed to hospital early hours of yesterday morning and…"

"Bloody hell, why are you here?"

"He's alright, teething actually, anyway, she flew off the handle at me and we haven't really spoken since."

"Shit, sorry, Jez, this is really playing on you, it is so clear see. You have gone from one of the happiest looking blokes around to the most miserable, she is sucking the life out of you, mate."

I felt a pinch of remorse, Seb didn't exactly have the smallest mouth around and Jude was my wife's best friend, "I'm alright," I lied.

"Yeah, pull the other one," he chided. "Let's go and get rat arsed tonight, you can stay at our place if you want."

"As much as I need to, I can't, I have a deadline and Mark is relying on me to be here tomorrow when Scorpio Marketing arrive, you know it's her biggest deal this year."

"Yes and ran by none other than Natasha Mason, Lord Nathan Mason's daughter."

"I didn't know that," I frowned, why didn't I know that?

"Yes and she is stunning, I mean, I might actually have a problem with her." He grinned.

"Seb, mate, you are losing your looks and I hate to tell you this, but all those booze ups you go on, they are showing on your waistline, look at that podge." I joked and poked him in his tummy. He hadn't put that much on, but he did fancy himself and needed to be taken down a peg or two, "Don't forget Jude has that meat grinder," I added.

"Good point." He chuckled as we walked into the office.

I already felt better and the guilt I had for not even saying goodbye to my wife was beginning to fade. I'd be fine until five, and then I'd have to go and face her again.

Three

Kelsey

Waking up alone in my bed was horrible, there is no other way to describe it. What was wrong with me? Of course I didn't think Harrison's fever was Jeremy's fault, still, I let my mouth runaway and I more or less accused him of forcing me to go out and leave him.

Harrison still slept soundly in his bed so I took a shower and got dressed. After drying my hair, he woke bright eyed and talking away. For his age he actually spoke really well, I had to remember he was not a baby anymore, in fact her was walking and talking and the one thing I wanted to do over the summer was potty train him. Six weeks in Southampton hospital put pay to that. Mum said I had put too much pressure on myself, he was barely two, I had time. Jeremy had mentioned it though, the last time we went shopping and I suppose it would be cheaper if I could get him clean and dry during the day at least.

I decided that after breakfast we would go and see her, I hadn't in a few weeks and I suppose you could say I needed a sympathetic ear. Jude had made it perfectly clear that I was not to call her, she had been a bitch to me for the last time, I was certain of that.

My mother was pleased to see us, but upset that I hadn't called her to let her know we had to visit the hospital again. Dave played with Harrison while we talked over a cup of tea. I felt like it had been months since I actually sat and talked to anyone. My life had become incredibly lonely and I knew that pushing Jeremy away wasn't helping, but I missed my friends too, missed my job and missed the wages at the end of the month,

"Maybe you should think about going back part-time," Mum suggested.

"Child care costs would probably take every penny I'd earn." I grumbled.

"Are you short of money, love?"

"No, no we're fine, Dad's money is building in savings now. Jeremy's wages cover the mortgage, we are coping financially, it's just emotionally. I just feel insignificant, with everything." A tear dripped from my eye and splashed on the back of my hand. It was hard to admit I was losing this battle, which I was failing as both a mother and a wife.

We stayed for lunch, Mum's home-made soup was always the best and with bread rolls soaking up the soup, Harrison ate a huge bowl full. After lunch we headed for the supermarket to do a grocery shop, I wanted to cook Jeremy a nice meal. I wanted to make it up to him, but I feared we were already too far down a road neither of us wanted to be on.

I got some chicken breast and peppers, some gluten free rice and some new Cajun spices. When we got home I began cooking while Harrison slept the afternoon away. I checked my mobile phone several times and he hadn't even sent a text, he must have been so angry at me and I didn't blame him. I had to take responsibility for this.

At seven Jeremy still hadn't arrived home. When I tried to call him I got his voice mail and the office phone lines were closed. I bathed Harrison and fed him pasta before he went to bed at eight-thirty. At nine o'clock I called his phone one more time,

"I'm on my way home," he barked after only one ring.

"Where have you been?" I asked.

"Working, I'm driving, I'll see you soon." He answered abruptly and ended the call. He sounded furious, maybe I had blamed him for the last time, maybe he was late because he was with Seb arranging to move in with them. Maybe I wasn't worth it anymore.

My hands began to shake, I wasn't cold, it was through fear, the fear that he might just say those words that would crush me, the words I dreaded to hear. I was so lucky to have found him, but we were as fragile as glass and I seriously didn't know how much more we could withstand before smashing into smithereens.

I cleaned the living room and made sure all of Harrison's toys were put away. Thinking that he would calm down if he saw how tidy the house was. I ran to the bathroom and pulled the hairband out of my hair and brushed it straight. I didn't want to put on makeup, I was close enough to crying and the last thing I needed was black streaks streaming my face.

As I stepped back into the living room flashlights lit it up, a car had driven onto the driveway. I sat on the couch and tucked my legs under me, lifted the remote of the TV and switched it on. I heard his car door slam shut and it made me jump, my palms began to sweat with anxiety and I could see my body quivering. The front door opened and closed quietly, Jeremy walked into the lounge with his work bag on his shoulder and his light grey suit with a dark blue tie dangling loosely from his neck.

"I meant to call you, sorry." He grumbled.

"I just got worried," I admitted jamming my hands between my thighs to stop them shaking.

"How is Harry?" Usually I would correct him, but not tonight, I didn't want to upset him anymore.

"He's okay, I took him to my mum's and she gave us soup for lunch."

"Good," he nodded and removed his bag from his shoulder, "I'm going for a shower."

"Sure, uh, are you hungry? I made dinner, it might still be edible."

"I am as it happens, give me fifteen minutes." He replied. I nodded and waited for him to leave the room before breathing a sigh of relief. We were amicable, I could do amicable.

I served the vegetable rice and lay the marinated, steamed chicken on top. I placed the plates on the table and waited for him to come down. I could smell him before he entered the room, his deodorant's scent filled the house. His dark hair was still wet and he was wearing a pair of shorts and a t-shirt, silently, he sat at the table.

He lifted his fork and smiled slightly, "This looks nice."

"I saw it on a program last week and thought I'd give it a try."

He cut a piece of the meat and put the fork into his mouth, "Wow," he beamed, "this is really lovely, Kelse, really lovely."

"Good," I smiled and cut a piece for myself. He was right, the meat melted on my tongue, in fact the last time I ate something as nice was when we went to the World's End for our first date. "About the other night," I started.

"I don't want to talk about it," he stated and lifted his glass of water taking a long sip.

"But I was wrong and I want to apologise." I insisted.

"I told you, I am used to it."

"I know," I frowned, "I just, I don't have anyone else, Jeremy, I only have you. Jude hates my guts and Nicki rarely comes round or calls and I know that's my fault. No one wants to be around me right now and to tell you the truth, I don't even want to be around me. I haven't seen Stuart in months and I suppose if I can't talk to you then I have no one." I admitted. He just stared, "I miss what we had, I miss us."

"I miss us too," he sighed and placed his fork down.

"Every time I look at him I get so scared that I will lose him, lose that beautiful baby boy. It breaks my heart to think that he could die like Ben did. You have no idea what it was like to lose my little brother, to lose my son as well, that will destroy me."

"I get that, Kelse, I do, but you know what, he is my son too and I keep thinking that if I hadn't have been such an idiot and stressed you out in the start of the pregnancy, then maybe he would be alright now."

I shook my head, "He has the same thing that Ben did, I know nothing we did or didn't do made him ill, but he is and if we can't be strong for each other, no one else will." My eyes filled with tears.

Sympathy filled his eyes as he reached towards my hand, "We can't go on like this, love, we just can't." He said as his warm fingers touched mine.

"What are you saying?" I asked as fear began to writhe inside.

He stared for a few painful moments, "I think we rushed into everything and had we built on our relationship rather than jumping the gun and getting married so quickly, maybe we would be stronger now." I snatched my hand away and stood from the table. "Kelsey," he frowned.

"If you are planning on going, then go," I frowned.

"I'm not, I just think that…"

"We made a mistake, you are saying we shouldn't have got married, so that what, it would be easier for you to walk away when your baby wasn't born perfect?" I demanded angrily.

"You are putting words into my mouth," he groaned. "Christ, it's all or nothing with you, you don't give me a break, you are on my back constantly…"

"I'll give you a break," I snapped. "You can sleep in the sodding spare room from now on." I turned and left him at the table.

I ran up to our room and fell on the bed, burying my face in my pillow where I sobbed like a baby. He didn't want us anymore, this was his way of backing out of the marriage. But I knew all too well that I did this, I pushed him too far and now he was done with me.

"Kelsey, I didn't mean I don't want this, I love you. I love you and Harrison more than life." I felt him sit on the bed. "You know me, I am no quitter, but I am not too proud to admit that things have got on top of us and we are heading down that road if we don't do something about it." He placed his hand on my back, "I am not going anywhere, you might be a bitch and unreasonable and stubborn, but I knew all of that the day I married you." I turned over to face him. "I know our son is sick and he has what your brother had, but technology has come a long way, you heard what they said about this operation, it could stop it progressing and he will live a long and normal life."

"What if he dies during the operation?" I asked.

"He won't, he's a Buxton and we are as hard as nails." He moved up the bed and placed his hand at the side of my tear drenched face, "Things are going to change, we are going to start living again and I think you should go back to work, you can go part-time, we'll get an Au Pair or a nanny, or maybe your mum would look after him. You need your life back, love, you need your friends and we need to have at least one night out a week, to go to the pictures or to a show, anything, just some us time."

"And you don't want to leave me?" I asked.

"No, definitely not. You are my world, Mrs Buxton and I am not ready to throw the towel in yet." He moved towards my face and pressed his soft, succulent lips to mine, as we parted he touched his forehead to mine "How could I ever leave you?"

"At the moment, I would leave me," I admitted.

"Well, I don't want to. Now come on, our dinner is getting cold." He stood and held out his hand. I took his hand and allowed him to tow me down the stairs. The warmth excited me, I'll admit that.

Over the next few days' things improved. He was back to kissing me goodbye in the morning and texting me during the day and it made me feel good, really good. I scheduled a meeting about returning to work on a part-time basis and asked if my mum would watch Harrison while I attended the meeting.

"Ten till two and not a minute longer," Sue, my tall and blonde team leader stated.

"Are you sure?" I checked.

"Positive, we've missed you, but I know your little munchkin is poorly, so a few hours a day and if he has to go back in for whatever, then you can have as much time as you need."

"Wow, that's amazing, Sue, thank you."

"You are welcome, chick." She smiled.

I must admit, being back in the office, feeling the buzz as I walked through placed excitement in my belly. Shawna and Nicki smiled as I passed them, I wasn't sure if they were pleased to see me or not, I didn't care to be honest. The thought of normality excited me and had I not gone into the office, I would never have believed it was something I needed.

Mum and Dave had taken Harrison out for the day so I headed into Poole to shop for some new office clothes. I meandered through the Dolphin shopping centre and gazed at the rails of clothes, but nothing truly caught my eye. I got myself a coffee and sat on a bench watching everyone around me enjoy their lives, giggling and talking, just like they did that Saturday I bumped into the Jeremy before his wedding to Tara. Thinking back to how he held me one last time, or so I thought at that moment, crushed my heart. I couldn't lose him, but I wasn't certain that I would be able to hold on to him tight enough either.

"Kelsey?" a voice broke into my thoughts. I looked up, standing in front of me wearing a worn leather jacket and a reckless smile stood Stuart. His wheat coloured hair was much longer and he looked tired, but he was there, as if he knew I needed someone, he appeared. I stood from the seat and wrapped my arms around him. I hadn't seen him in months, I didn't even know if he knew about Harrison. "I just got back to Poole last night, how are you?" he asked into my hair. I pulled back from him and frowned. "What is it?"

"I don't want to burden you," I shrugged. "Where have you been?"

"Luke and I broke up about eight weeks ago, so I went home, well, I mean, back to Portsmouth for a while, but after a blazing row with the uh, 'Not my family anymore', I drove back last night."

"I didn't know you had broken up with Luke," I frowned, "I am so sorry and a lousy friend, no wonder they have all abandoned me."

"What do you mean?" he asked and sat back on the bench with me.

"I haven't seen Lou or Shawna in months, Nicki only bothers when Felix is working away and as for Jude, well, she has washed her hands of me." I explained. "Ever since Harrison was diagnosed I guess…"

"Diagnosed with what?" he asked.

"He has a bad heart, in laymen terms, he needs a new valve and they can't operate until he is three."

"Oh my God, Kelsey, I am so sorry, I didn't know. I have been so wrapped up in Luke drama I didn't realize that my best friend in the world needed me."

"It has to have been almost eighteen months since I last saw you. Still, you are here now," I took hold of his hand. "What happened with Luke?"

He looked around, "He was cheating on me, Kelsey, the whole time, he had some guy in London, the whole, '*I can't come out, it will ruin my family,*' thing was a lie. He had been out since he was sixteen according to his sister. So anyway, a guy called Adrian began calling him day and night, I got the number one day and lied about who I was and he told me that he and Luke had been, get this, engaged for three years and were adopting a baby from Thailand. Do I have *Gullible Prick* tattooed across my forehead?"

"What an arsehole," I grumbled as his eyes welled with tears.

"I waited for him to come down that weekend and I confronted him. He didn't deny it and said I was just a little south coast fun," he added. "He was my first boyfriend and I would have given him the world if I could." He sniffed.

"Oh, Stuart, that is horrible." I squeezed his hand. "Do you have your car?"

"No, I walked here from Lou's, I can't even move back in there, they have someone else there now. I slept in my car on their drive last night."

"Come on," I stood, "we're going back to my place, we'll figure something out, okay?" He nodded and walked back to my car with me.

I made us some tea and we sat in the living room talking the afternoon away. It was amazing to see him again and although his situation was pretty awful, he was back and I hadn't felt that good in weeks.

After a sandwich for lunch we sat around the dining table looking at pictures of Harrison and of our wedding. It seemed so long ago, I have never thought of myself as overly attractive, everyone said I looked stunning, and gazing at the pictures, I seemed to glow. Even with a bump in front of me, my hair stayed up and curled, my make-up was as flawless as when Serena put it on and my dress, my beautiful, oyster shell pink dress looked like something out of Hello magazine, with Jeremy on my arm, we could have passed as an A-list celebratory couple.

Of course we came across a picture of him with Luke, I watched as his eyes glassed over, I placed my hand on top of his,

A tear dripped from his eye, "What am I going to do, Kelsey? I don't have anywhere to live or anything."

"We'll sort something out, I have money, maybe we can find you a flat."

"I don't even have a job," he sighed and tossed the picture down on the pile. "They said I was too unreliable, who will give me a ruddy job now? I am screwed."

"I'll make us another drink," I frowned. "No more looking at these pictures, I am meant to be cheering you up, not send you into deep depression."

I left him at the table and put the kettle on, as I prepared the cups my mobile went off on the kitchen counter. I lifted it, Jeremy's amazing smile beamed at me, "Hello?"

"Hey, Kelse, look, I might be late tonight, I have that meeting set up for three, but chances are it will run over."

"Oh, right," I frowned, that would make three late nights then.

"Are you okay?"

"Yes," I lied.

"How did the meeting go?"

"Good, I just have to find a nursery that will take Harrison and then I can call them with a start date."

"That's great, love."

"Yeah, I uh, I better go, Stuart is here, he is a bit upset, so…"

"Where has he been?" he asked.

"Long story short, Luke is a lying, cheating piece of shit. I can tolerate most things, but a cheat, they are the lowest of the low." I spouted off. "He went home for a while."

"Poor bloke, well, give him my regards."

"I will, I might invite him to stay for dinner, he doesn't even have anywhere to live." I explained.

"Well, why doesn't he take the spare room for a few days, until he sorts something out?"

"Are you sure?" I checked.

"Yes, he's a mate and he'll be company for you."

"Okay," I smiled, excited by the concept, "thank you."

"You don't have to thank me, it's your house too. Look, I should go, I love you, Mrs Buxton."

"I love you too," I replied and ended the call.

Four

Jeremy

I didn't see it as lying, more of a bend of the truth sort of thing. I was working in a sense, I just had to meet Natasha Mason for dinner for the third time that week and discuss the newly amended contracts. But if I had told Kelsey it was for dinner and with another woman, though completely innocent, she would read too much into it and we'd be fighting again. Things were better and I saw no need to add fuel to a fire for no good reason.

The relief I felt to hear Stuart was back on the scene, was immense. She seemed to have lost all contact with her friends and he was definitely needed. She had too much time to sit around and wallow and I knew Stuart wouldn't allow that. I hadn't seen him yet, but he had apparently accepted our offer to move in for a while and I knew she needed the company. So now I could go out and not feel so guilty for having a pleasant evening.

The first dinner was extremely business like, Natasha, for want of a better word, was a flirt. She was stunningly beautiful and the thought of that alone made my wedding ring feel suddenly tighter. She was almost six feet tall with chestnut brown hair that she wore up in many different styles. Her eyes were like frosted ice, light blue with a subtle sparkle and long dark eyelashes. Her cherry red lips glistened whenever she spoke and her pure white teeth were almost blinding. She looked like Audrey Hepburn in that Galaxy chocolate advert on TV. She was going to be my new boss and I couldn't say no to meeting her, it would have been rude and may have given her the wrong impression.

We arranged to meet at the Crown Hotel in Blandford again, it was a nice place, the food tasted pretty good, although not as nice as Felix's food, but they were able to meet my dietary limitations, which was something most restaurants lacked. She had texted me and said she was driving in from Shaftesbury, so to meet her there at six-thirty.

As I sat at the table waiting for her to arrive, I told myself I had to be gone by ten at the latest, the drive back to Branksome would take almost an hour. Kelsey would be up waiting, so alcohol was a definite no too, besides, I did want to go home to my wife, I was shattered and needed to go to bed.

I began reading over the contracts while waiting for Natasha to arrive, sipping iced water with a slice of lime in, I crunched on an ice-cube as starvation peaked that day. I had skipped lunch amending the contacts, so was ravenous by the time she arrived fifteen minutes late.

"Please tell me you are not drinking water again," she said from my side. I looked up from the papers and she smiled. She was wearing a tight fitting black dress and high heeled, knee length boots.

"I have to drive home, remember?" I muttered.

"You can have one drink," she said sitting opposite me.

"No, not me, I don't drive if I even have a sip. I can't lose my license." I responded.

"I admire your discipline," she grinned revealing those knock out teeth.

"I am not disciplined, just not stupid." I countered.

She sat opposite me and removed her coat. Her dress had thin straps and a thin row of diamantes around them. "So, how's the little wife?" she asked sarcastically.

I wanted to snap at her, but she could be the biggest deal the company had, I doubted they'd like it if I lost the contract for them, "She's great actually. She's returning to work and I know it will do her the world of good."

"Mmm, I am sure it will." She looked over at the waiter and he came over. She ordered herself a large glass of wine and asked for the menu. To be honest, it was the third time we had eaten there this week and I was beginning to wonder if she was ever going to agree to sign these contracts.

During the meal she asked how I met Kelsey and I told her about the party and how Tara almost ruined my life. I didn't want to go into the details of what happened between us leading up to the wedding or in deed how hard it has been since Harry was diagnosed with his heart problem. I moved away from talking about my family and changed the subject many times, but she seemed intrigued. She kept asking about all sorts of things, about Kelsey and if she had got her pre-baby body back. Of course she had, except her boobs were more voluptuous, she had more than a handful now, but that was something I would never admit to Natasha.

"I hear you went to Eton," she beamed and sipped at her fourth glass of wine.

"Yes," I smiled slightly, "its where my parents sent me after we returned from the States."

She swallowed another sip of wine, "Mmm, I had a boyfriend that went there once, Oscar Pembroke-Wilson."

"Ozzy? Really, you went out with Ozzy Wilson?"

"Yes, for about three years in the end, we even got engaged for a while." She nodded and put her glass down.

"Wow," I grinned, "so how is Ozzy?"

"Dead," she frowned staring at her glass for a few moments.

"What?" I asked, shocked.

"Dead, he died about two years ago, skiing in the Alps. He broke his neck and died while being airlifted to hospital."

I didn't know what to say, "Bloody hell," I sighed, "I am so sorry."

"Yes, well, he loved to ski," she muttered and sipped her wine again. "We had been broken up about three years before his accident; he had some Swiss floozy on his arm by then." She almost looked upset. "Oh no, I am so sorry," she frowned again looking over my shoulder. I turned my head, it was almost ten. "I hope Kelly is okay."

"Kelsey," I corrected, "she'll be fine," I stood, "but I had better go, I have work again in the morning."

"I'll drop by the office at eleven with these contracts if that's okay?"

"Great," I smiled and handed the company credit card to the waiter. He returned and handed me the card. As I turned to leave, Natasha stood and stumbled into the table.

"Whoops!"

"Are you alright?" I asked her as I put on my jacket.

"Just a little tipsy," she giggled.

I couldn't leave her in that state. "Do you want me to take you to your hotel?"

"I'm staying here, but you could walk me up to my room."

I led her out to the stairs and walked beside her as she climbed them slowly. I could see she wasn't steady on her feet at all as she staggered down the hall.

At her room door she turned and smiled, "You are a real gentleman, Mr Buxton."

"Thanks," I shrugged. She unlocked her door. "Goodnight, Natasha."

"Goodnight," she said as she stumbled over on the side of her boot. Crashing into me, her hands rested on my chest and she gazed into my eyes,

"Okay?" I checked as I steadied her and switched on the light in her room.

"Yes, I am going to bed," she announced and walked into the room. I closed the door and hurried out to my car.

Kelsey was going to kill me.

When I got home the house was in darkness, this could mean one of two things, she was either asleep, which would be great, but at almost eleven I doubted it, or as my best guess she was more than likely sat in bed reading or something.

I crept through the house up to our room and pushed open the door, thankful that she was asleep. I undressed and brushed my teeth in the bathroom before slowly and gently crawling between the sheets. I rested my head against the pillow and closed my eyes.

"You're late," she said sourly in the darkness.

"I know, I'm sorry."

"Do I need to speak with your boss?"

"I'm not seven, Kelse." I snapped.

"I was joking," she sighed and turned away from me. Great, the cold shoulder again, I knew I deserved it though.

It didn't take me long to fall asleep and in true alarm clock nature, when it rang out, I didn't feel like I had even slept for an hour. I sat up in the darkness of our room and I could feel that I was being watched.

"Is this going to be permanent?" she asked quietly as I pulled my trousers up my legs and fastened them.

"What?" I asked and sat on the side of the bed.

"The late nights, are these your new hours or something?"

"Of course not, I just had to meet with Natasha Mason a few times, we are trying to get her to agree to some contracts, but they needed editing." I explained pulling on my socks.

"It just feels like we are going back to how it was before and... did you say Natasha Mason? As in the 'A' lister who part-owns some of the main magazines in London?"

"Yes, and this would be huge for us, not to mention that I could actually get a promotion out of it. So, if I have to work late a few times a week, I'm sorry but I am going to do it."

"I thought you said you didn't care about money," she grumbled and flicked on the bed side lamp.

"I don't, but what I do care about is my son, our son. I want to get him seen by a private doctor and pay for him to have the best medical help he can get. There is nothing wrong with the hospitals or doctors, but I can't help feeling that if we were paying for more, we'd get more." Her eyes filled with tears, I reached toward her and took her warm hand in mine.

"I thought it was because you didn't want to come home to us," she sniffed.

"Never," I smiled slightly. "I will be home on time tonight, I promise." I leaned towards her and kissed her tenderly. "I love you, wife."

"I love you too, husband." She croaked. I pressed my hand against the side of her face and wiped away her tears with my thumb. "It will be okay, sweetheart." She nodded her head and tried to smile. "I should go, get some sleep."

"I'm awake now," she said letting my hand go. "Stuart is coming here today, he will stay for a week and promises to find somewhere soon."

"He can stay for as long as he needs to." I stated standing from the bed and tying my tie.

"I'll tell him then."

I lifted my suit jacket from the chair and slipped my feet into my brown brogues. "I will see you later, okay?"

She nodded, "I'll make something nice for dinner."

"Perfect." I smiled and left her in bed.

My car took a while to de-mist, the cooler nights caused the windows to mist up and I couldn't go anywhere until they were clear. I listened to Richard and Zoe on Heart breakfast radio talk and giggle in between songs, they certainly gave me something to smile about on my way to work in the mornings. I loved the songs too, especially the older tunes reminding me of my Eton days and nights, parties in my dorm room and when we snuck off to a local pub and got smashed on cider. Those were the days, mind you, had I known how life would have ended up, I might have worked harder and attempted to do the degree I always wanted. Maybe then I wouldn't be working for the man, he would, in fact, be working for me.

Finally, after twenty-five minutes, I could see to drive and make the seventeen mile drive out to North Dorset, Blandford. The Evoque was not a cheap car, but the demister was bloody crap, if I am honest. Still, I loved my car and as I was slightly excited by the concept that Natasha would actually sign the contracts for us to do her copy editing, it put a spring in my step. This would be a huge company boost and I knew it meant a lot to all of us who had worked on the pitch and the bidding.

Arriving at work with my black, machine Costa coffee from the petrol station in my hand, Gregg Anderson, from Final Editing, greeted me at the front door with a cocky smile.

"How was your date?" he asked pulling the door open.

"What date?" I frowned into his brown eyes.

"With Natasha Mason," he shrugged.

I wasn't aware that it had spread around my team, "It wasn't a date, it was a business meal." I corrected as I walked inside.

He smirked slightly, "Oh, I heard it was something more."

"You came to the evening do at my wedding, Gregg. I don't cheat on my wife, I will never cheat on my wife. Not for a job or anything else."

"Sorry, mate, but that's all I have been told."

"From who?"

"Doesn't matter, the whole office is talking about it," he added. "I have to go, I'll see you later."

I watched him leave and headed into the office through the key coded door. I felt like my office was watching my every move as I walked in. Eyes followed me to my desk and continued to stare as I placed my cup down. I lifted my head at Vanessa and Sian snickering behind me.

"What's your problem?" I asked. They both shrugged and looked away.

"Jeremy?" Mark, manager called over to me from his door, "Can I have a word?" Gazing around at them as I passed, I left my desk and walked towards his small office at the back. "Close the door," he said I entered the room. "Have a seat." He added as I turned to face him. He looked tired, I guessed the stress of this deal was getting to him. "So?" he said sweeping a hand over his dark, brown hair.

I stared into his brown eyes, "So?" I grimaced heavily as I sat in front of him.

He paused briefly, "I'll come right out and ask then. Do I need to be aware of any conflict of interest between you and Miss Mason?"

"What? No!" I answered.

"Are you certain?"

"I am positive, Mark. I would never do that to Kelsey for one thing, besides, I don't even think of her that way." I insisted. "Who told you otherwise?" I asked.

"She did." He replied bluntly.

"What?" I stood. "Why would she...? Look, I met her at the Crown, we had a meal, she drank a bottle and a half of wine and I drank water, then after the meal I helped her to her room."

"And then?"

My forehead had dampened and my ties felt suddenly tighter, why did I feel guilty? "Nothing," I answered, "I left her in her room and went home to my wife and child."

"So, you didn't go into her room at all?" he checked.

"Absolutely not," I affirmed. "I flicked on the light from the doorway and closed the door on her. As far as I was aware she was going to bed. I did not go into her room nor did I touch her or anything like that." I stated in certainty. He sat back in his chair and touched his fingertips together while staring at me. "Is this what they all think?" I asked. "I have been married for just over two years, if you knew what I went through with Kelsey to win her; you would see that I am not lying at all."

"I know what you went through, I saw the mess you were in which is why I am asking you, man to man." He explained. "I am not accusing you; I just needed to know your side before I went accusing anyone."

"Can you do me a favour then?" I asked.

"Okay," he frowned.

"Put someone else on the account. I would rather not have any more contact with her if this is what she is like. I won't work with liars."

He sat forward, "But you worked so hard on this, it would be unfair to give it to someone else in the closing stages."

"Please, Mark. If Kelsey got wind of this, I could kiss my marriage goodbye. It's been pretty fragile since Harry was diagnosed, this would push her over the edge."

"I think you should talk to Kelsey first and if she wants you off the account I will move you." He lifted his glass of water, "Miss Mason has postponed coming in today until next week, something came up. Look, its Friday, take the day off and go out with your family. Make the most of the sun while we still have it and enjoy an extended weekend." He took a mouthful of water and set the glass down.

"Are you sure?"

He nodded as he swallowed, "Yes, go and relax, Jeremy; you look tired and I know you'll let this bug you until it's sorted out."

"But won't it look like I have something to hide, if I just go, I mean?" I queried.

He nodded. "Okay, how about I send you out, you go back to your desk and I'll come and ask you to go out for me, will that be better?"

I smiled and nodded, I couldn't wait to tell Kelsey that we had three days together, "Thanks, Mark."

"Don't let on to anyone, they'll think I've gone soft."

"I won't." I promised and left his office.

With the same gazing eyes, I braved the office. I sat at my desk and logged into my computer. It always took a while to fire up in the morning, I had a few things I wanted to check and sift through my new e-mails and check if any needed forwarding to my personal account at home. I had seven new messages to read through, though the first knocked me off balance.

'Meet me at the hotel or I will tell everyone what you did.' It was from Natasha.

I replied,
'What I did??? You and I both know that I took you back to your room and left.'

'Well, maybe if that little wife of yours is as delicate as you said, she'd believe me if I told her differently.' She responded.

I glanced around quickly at the office, Seb was glaring at me, why did I feel so guilty, I had done nothing wrong? *'Why are you doing this?'* I typed as sweat began to form on my forehead.

'You have an hour, if you come I will tell you, if you don't, me and Mrs Buxton will be having a conversation.'

'Fine, but I'll warn you, I am fucking pissed off now!!!' I hammered into my keyboard.

"You alright, mate?" Seb called over to me.
"Yes," I lied, "why?"
"The colour has drained from your face," he frowned, "are you sure?"
"Yeah, just feeling a bit off today." The lies were falling from my mouth, what the hell was going on and why would she want to do this?
"Jeremy?" Mike called out. "I need you to go to Dorchester for me."
"Okay," I switched off my screen.
"Great, here's the list, you might have to go into Poole too, I need some stuff from Staples."

"I'm on it." I promised and stood from my chair. I grabbed the list from Mark and hurried out of the office and their gawping eyes.

I roared out of the carpark on the main road, what a bitch, if Kelsey found out about this, I would lose her and Harry. I had to set her straight.

Five

Kelsey

After Jeremy left I got up and changed the bed in the spare room. We had painted the house mostly magnolia. It looked clean and was natural so we could buy accessories of different colours in each of the rooms. It just so happened that I decided on teal for that room. It had teal curtains and lamp shades, a teal bedspread and cream carpet. The solid pine wardrobe and dressing table was from my flat and the chair in the corner belonged to Jeremy's mum.

Our room was cream, black and red, I liked the modern image it gave the room and with the money we had been given as wedding presents; we bought new furniture and a new bed. In Harrison's room we had gone with monkeys, he loved them, they always made him laugh and we put transfers of them all over the walls. It looked so cute.

I thought that with Stuart moving in, he was going to need a clean and fresh bed to sleep in so changed the teal quilt cover for a beige one. I was so excited that I could tell him he could stay as long as he needed to. He had commented on how nice the house was. I took pride in my home and tried to keep it as clean and tidy as possible. We had two black leather couches in the living room, I don't know why, but I added a little green to that room, I suppose it reminded me of the grass in the summer.

The dining room was burgundy and cream and the kitchen was black and white like the two bathrooms we had. At the back of the house we had a small office where Jeremy worked on contracts and played Sims on his computer, he made out he was working, but I knew what he was up to. The computer was provided by his company and a huge black leather chair behind the antique desk my mum restored and gave us. His chair was the only bit of furniture he owned when I met him. It came from America and had been in every home he'd had. We'd had a lot of fun on that chair, that's all I am telling you.

The house, I suppose, was plain looking, but it was how I wanted it, clean and clutter free. We couldn't have too much furniture because of Harrison, dust irritated his chest, so the minimalist look was not only a choice, it was a necessity.

Harrison woke up as bright as a button. His bright, blue eyes sparkled as I lifted him out of his bed. I carried him down to the dining room and sat him in his high chair feeding him his breakfast. After he ate his toast I gave him a bath, he loved bubbles in the water. We played cars on the living room rug for a few hours, I enjoyed playing with him, I felt that every moment with Harrison was so precious. He loved cars and pushed them around making raspberry noises and dribbling down his front.

Just after eleven the front doorbell rang, I raced to the door and pulled it open. Stuart smiled recklessly,
"Come in," I told him. Carrying a couple of bags, he followed me into the living room. I put Harrison in his playpen and turned to him.
"You have a cage for you baby?" he smiled.
"It's not a cage it's a playpen and he loves it in there, plus I don't have to worry about him climbing when I am trying to sort the house out." I explained.
"I am only playing, Kelse," he grinned.
"Come on, I'll show you to your room."

I led him up the stairs and into the now very bland looking, beige room. He placed his bags on the bed and smiled slightly.
"You can stay for as long as you need, Jeremy suggested you stay until you are back on your feet."
"Are you sure?"
"Yes," I smiled, "it is going to be amazing having you here." I added throwing my arms around him and hugging him tightly.
"Steady on, love," he chuckled.
"I have missed you, so much."
"I missed you too and if I wasn't so stubborn, I would never have left in the first place."
"You're here now," I sniffed pulling back from his arms.
"Kelsey, what's wrong?"

I wanted to tell him, I really did, but he had just got there and with the weight of the world on his shoulders, he didn't need my worries too. "I'm fine," I lied, "just thrilled that you are here."

"You still can't lie to me, love," he said softly. "Come on, let's get a cuppa and talk rent money, then you can tell me everything."

"I don't want rent money from you," I grimaced.

"Well, I'll pay in babysitting then, I will not stay here and not pay my way, I am proud like that."

I put Harrison to bed for a nap after his spaghetti hoops lunch and while I was upstairs, Stuart made more tea. I sat with him on the sofa and we talked, really talked. I told him of my concerns that Jeremy wanted to leave me; that he'd finally had enough and had given up on us. I admitted how I hadn't been much of a wife recently and of my fight with Jude.

"Well, Jude is a first class bitch, we both know that. But there is no way Jez would leave you, Kelsey."

"Okay, so what about his working late? Or the way he talks to me sometimes? I try to make it up to him, but for what? I can't lose him, Stuart, I can't." I sniffed as a tear trickled down my cheek.

"When was the last time you two had some time together?" he asked. "I don't mean the occasional romp either." He added.

"Honestly?" I checked, he nodded, "I don't remember, probably before Harrison was born, no actually, my mum had him a couple of times before he got sick."

"Right then, I am here now, so you two can have a bit of grown-up time."

Panic struck my heart, "No, it's okay."

"Don't you trust me to look after Harrison for you?" he questioned, I just frowned at him. "I would call you if I needed you," he assured.

"I'll think about it," I promised. As if, the last time I left him he ended up in the hospital again. No way!

That afternoon we took Harrison to Poole Park. We fed the ducks and walked around the lake, Stuart took him on the train and took pictures with my phone. We then went to the swing park so he could play. Stuart pushed him on the swing and I honestly don't remember him laughing so much. It was nice to see him happy and wondered why a child so young always seemed so worried, then of course it hit me, the tension between Jeremy and I was playing on our son, what sort of parents did that to their children?

I realized that Jeremy hadn't even sent me a text, much less a phone call at lunch time like he normally did. I sent him a quick text of a picture of Harrison on the train with Stuart and to ask if he was okay, I didn't want him to think I was checking up on him again and cause another argument.

'Aww that's cute. Yes, I'm fine, just bus.' he text back.

'He loved it on the train. We missed you though, we love you.' I replied. He didn't respond. I wondered what had upset him this time, there had to be something, he had never been this blunt even when he was angry at me.

On the way out of the park Stuart asked if I was okay, I lied and said yes. We stopped at my mum's for a cuppa and she made a huge fuss of Stuart. Mum ended up making sandwiches for us and Harrison lapped up the attention he was getting by all of us.

After lunch, while I helped mum wash up my phone buzzed in my pocket. It was a text from Jude,

'I'm sorry!!!' was all it said.

Instead of replying I dialled her number and called her. She answered after only one ring,

"I am a selfish, pig-headed bitch and I don't deserve your friendship, but you have to believe me, Kelse, I do not think you are a bad mother or wife, I never will."

"Okay," I frowned.

"No, you're right, I should be begging on my knees because I haven't been much of a friend recently. It's all this wedding bullshit and I just wish I married Seb in Oz when he asked me now."

"Jude, it's…"

"Yes, Seb asked me to marry him out there, I would have, but I thought I could not marry him without my best friend there. We've decided to get married in April, at Buxton Manor, I am not running up to Gretna Green or anywhere else, if I can't get married with my best friend at my side, then I am not getting married at all."

"Jude, will you just let me get a word in?" I pleaded.

"Of course, sorry."

"Everything you said Saturday night was accurate, no one wants to be around me because I have been an obsessive, controlling cow and let's face it who wants to be around a drama queen."

"You are not a drama queen, your baby is sick and I should support you, not bloody fight with you. Do you forgive me?"

"Of course, but there is…"

"Will you be my bridesmaid? I mean, my Maid of Honour?"

"Yes," I smiled, "I'd love to, but no pink and no green."

"With my hair colouring," she chuckled. "Thank you," she added.

"No, Jude, thank you. You always manage to kick me up the arse when I need it."

"We are throwing an official engagement party on Halloween, please tell me you and Jez will come, I know Seb would want his best man there."

"Best man?" I smiled.

"Shit, yes, but he hasn't asked him yet, don't let on, will you?"

"I won't," I promised.

"So you'll come?"

"If my mum can have Harry for the night then yes, oh, and uh, Stuart's back."

"Oh my God, really?"

"So, is he invited too?"

"Definitely," she then went on to talk about costumes for the party to piss Lord and Lady Buxton off, they wanted to get Hello and OK to the party and Jude being Jude wanted a Fright Fest. Personally, I thought it was a great idea and it would bring the Buxtons down a peg or two. Not that I had any intention of going dressed up. She said how she had invited Hermione, Elle and Julian, and I knew Jeremy would love to see them all again.

I told Stuart about the party and mum and Dave jumped at the chance of babysitting Harrison. All I had to do now was convince Jeremy that even though the party was an engagement, a fancy dress Halloween party was on the cards and I couldn't wait to be with the old gang again.

On the way back to the house we stopped at Tesco's supermarket and did a bit of grocery shopping. Harrison needed some more pull-ups and we looked at some of the costumes they had on display for Halloween. Stuart bought some toys for Harrison, he felt bad for not getting him anything for his birthday. I tried to put him off, but he insisted. A battle I couldn't win.

Arriving back at our house to Jeremy's car parked on the drive put excitement in my belly. I felt like I did when we first met, I don't know why, but all of the darkness that had consumed me for so long seemed to have been washed away. Yes, Harrison was still sick, but I didn't feel so lonely or useless.

When we got inside, I gave Jeremy a huge hug, pulling him into my arms and holding him tightly. He pecked my lips lightly and it set a fire burning inside. I had so much to tell him. He looked tired and I was so pleased that Mark rewarded him for all the hours he had put in that week. He deserved it.

Six

Jeremy

I arrived at the Crown Hotel to discover Natasha, dressed in blue jeans and a white, see-through shirt, I could see her lace bra under her shirt and that she was cold. Her hair was tied up in a loose ponytail and she had a lighter pink lipstick on as opposed to the bright red she usually wore. She was leaning against the post of the gate to the car park with her head resting on her hand, looking like butter wouldn't melt in her mouth, but I now knew differently. Anger seeped through my veins, I would not be held to ransom, not by her or anyone else.

I parked my car and just as I unclicked my seat belt she climbed in beside me. Her sweet smelling perfume hit the back of my throat,

"Get out of my car," I ordered.

"Drive," she stated, ignoring my order. I rolled my eyes and sighed. "You don't want anyone to hear what I have to say, so I suggest you drive away from here and find us somewhere we can talk without worrying about who can see us."

"What do you want, Natasha?" I demanded impatiently.

"Drive and I will tell you."

I drove us out of the town centre towards the North Dorset council offices. I knew there was a huge car park there and that part of it was surrounded by trees. She didn't look too impressed and I didn't care. The old red brick building was directly ahead of us as we drove in. I followed the arrows around the car park and came to a stop near some trees.

"Where are we?" she asked.

"Somewhere secluded enough that they won't hear me yelling at you, but public enough that I could find witnesses if you tried to pull any 'He's attacking me' shit."

"Jeremy, what sort of girl do you take me for?"

"The kind of girl who wants to wreck a home and a marriage," I retorted.

"I don't want to wreck your marriage, but I will if you don't give me what I want." She replied smartly.

"And I will ask again, what do you want, Natasha?"

"You, Jeremy, I want to feel your hands on my body. I want to have you at my mercy, Jeremy Buxton, I want you to fuck me like your life depended on it."

I almost laughed, but when I looked at her I could see she was serious, "Why?"

"Have you seen yourself? It would be an absolute crime to sell your soul to just one girl, one that doesn't deserve you. You are too good for her, you have always been too good for her."

"How do you know? Kelsey is the most amazing woman I know, she is kind and considerate, she cares and God knows why, but she loves me. I don't need anyone else, she is all I need and she is all I want."

"Are you refusing me?" she asked.

"Yes I am," I affirmed adamantly.

"You should know I always get what I want." She smirked.

"That makes two of us," I scoffed.

"I don't think you understand," she frowned.

"Oh I do, you can't get your own man, so you want to blackmail me into having an affair with you." I started my engine.

"It's easy to think that, plus I can have any man I want."

"Not this man," I snapped.

"Fine, have it your way, I am sure Kelsey will want to know about our little meeting today, to discuss what happened between us last night."

"Nothing happened," I frowned and began driving. "I am taking you back to your hotel, this conversation is over."

"And what about your job, do you really want to be responsible for The Press to lose this contract because of your reluctance to co-operate?"

"Mark is on my side," I shrugged.

"He is at the moment." She retorted as I pulled out onto the road. What the hell was this woman, a bloody bunny boiler? "So, you are prepared to throw away your career and marriage?"

"Kelsey would believe me, she trusts me."

"Really?"

"Yes, really."

"Well, I guess we'll find out, won't we?" she smirked again.

"This is sexual harassment, I could have you in court." I warned.

"And who would they believe more? You, a diplomat's kid with more notches in his bed post than he has had hot dinners, how many women have you had, Jeremy?"

"Kelsey knows what I was like, I have told her everything."

"So, what about Marni, the girl you slept with while she was away on her friend's hen weekend in Majorca, does she know about her? Or the one just after you broke up with her and she fled back to Poole. Maybe I should tell her about Simone too, remember Simone? You probably don't, you were so drunk a few nights before your wedding to Tara, I doubt you remember her."

"There was no Simone," I frowned.

"There was, and do you want to know how I know about her? She is my cousin."

"That doesn't mean a thing," I shrugged.

"Stop the car and I will show you." I pulled over to the side of the road and stopped as she lifted her phone from her bag. She showed a picture of me naked on a bed with a dark haired girl on top of me, I pulled the phone from her hand. "Don't worry, if you delete them, I have copies." I swiped my thumb over the screen, picture after picture. Shit! "Believe me now, look at the date? That was the Wednesday night before the wedding. So, you must be wondering how I got this picture. Well, my cousin went to school with one Hermione Buxton and she called in a favour after Kelsey tried to get Tara to confess to the baby not being yours. Ruby, my cousin and her younger sister, Simone and I met at a club in Bournemouth, we found you and you went back to Simone's hotel room and had sex with her, Ruby and I took pictures."

"You have seriously lost the plot, you know that?" I shook my head and handed the phone back to her.

"If Tara still didn't admit it about the baby, we were going to show her dad the pictures of you and Simone." She replaced her phone back into her bag. "Go home to your wife and try and look her in the eye now. You are not so innocent, Jeremy and if I don't get what I want, then everything will come out, including the pictures I have of you."

I had nothing, I literally had nothing I could say. I felt sick and my hands began to tremble. Kelsey would go crazy. I could have given her something, not to mention that the night of my stag do I turned up at her flat rat-arsed and we had un-protected sex on her couch. After we lost the baby, she was tested for all of this diseases and I could have been the one to give them to her, I could have caused her to lose the baby.

"Not so cocky now, are you, Jeremy?" she stated smugly.

I began driving again, allowing my temper to filter through my lungs, "My son is sick, do you get that, you selfish bitch?" I roared. "You threaten me, to destroy my marriage and all because you want me to have sex you. Well, you know what; you can go and fuck yourself. I am not playing this game. I will tell Kelsey everything and then you will have nothing on me, nothing at all."

I sped through the streets of Blandford all the way to her hotel. I parked the car and she un-clipped her seatbelt.

"It's a shame, because I think I would have liked working with you."

"Well, it's just a job," I lied.

She leaned towards me and I thought she was going to kiss me. I moved my head back so she couldn't reach my lips, but in one movement, she grabbed hold of my crutch, rubbing her hand up and down while pushing her breasts into my arm.

"Feel that?" she said breathlessly as she rubbed, I'm a man, of course I responded, I couldn't not respond; it was rough and forceful, but didn't stop my erection forming. "You want this, you want me, you know you do." She continued and pressed her lips to my neck.

"Stop," I protested and tried to push her off. I tried to fight it, to not let her have this control over me, this power, but the more she rubbed, the harder it got until the pain of holding it in became excruciating. My head almost exploded with pressure and sweat covered my forehead. I sucked hard on the warm air in the car, my throat felt so coarse and dry, I could barely breathe until I could fight it no more, I had to let it go. The relief was instant and immense, but the shame I felt smothered me just as quickly. The warmth in my lap soon cooled as the throbbing and pain appeased.

As she removed her hand she smiled smugly, "There is plenty more where that came from." Fury burned at my soul, nothing had ever had me wanting to hit a woman before in my life, but this, this was close. For her safety and my pride, I needed to get away from there.

"Get out of my car, now," I ordered angrily.

"Don't you want to come up to my room and see what will happen next?" she asked coyly.

"No, get the fuck out of my car, now." I yelled.

"Fine," she sighed and sat back in her seat. "Call me if you reconsider, if I don't hear from you by Monday morning, I'll assume you will be resigning from your job and expecting some photographs in the post. I mean it, Jeremy, it doesn't have to be this way."

"Get out!" I roared.

She climbed out of the car and closed the door. I sat there with a wet and sticky lap feeling totally violated and weak. How could I let her do that to me? How could I tell Kelsey now, she'd never believe me, with my track record, who would?

During my drive home I went from feeling sick to feeling disgusted. I shouldn't have agreed to meet her. I should have said no. I already had Mark on my side and now all I did was add fuel to the fire. This was going to spiral and I knew Kelsey would never truly understand that I was in fact innocent in all of this.

My grey trousers had a dark grey patch that needed covering and as I drove onto my drive, relief filled my body, Kelsey was out. I still removed my suit jacket and held it in front of me as I hurried into the house. God only knows what the neighbours would think if they saw me.

I ran up to my room and stripped of my clothes, jumped into the shower and tried in vain to wash away her violation. Though my body was clean, I didn't feel clean and as I climbed out of the shower I wrapped a towel around my waste and gazed at the mirror. Who would believe me? Who would listen to a man? Women do not normally sexually assault men, but she did, so she made me ejaculate, it wasn't an orgasm, there is no way I would let her own that.

I wiped the steam from the mirror and caught one glimpse of my face as vomit shot up my throat; I barely made it to the toilet before violently heaving my guts up. I knew I needed to man up, I needed to not let this destroy me or our marriage, but first I had to stop her, trouble was, I had no idea of how or what to do and worse than that, time, like grains of sand in an hourglass, seemed to be slipping through my fingers.

Dressed in clean jeans and a hoody, I hurried down the stairs with my clothes and towel tucked under my arm. I put them in the washing machine and switched it on, then made myself a cup of black coffee and with it shaking in my hand, I sat on the couch.

I could do this, I could pretend everything was okay, I could, I knew I could, but for how long? Kelsey knew me better than I knew myself and with our already strained relationship, I doubted we would survive this. The one thing she hated more than anything was a cheat, okay, I didn't take Natasha to bed like she wanted, but she touched me and in the eyes of anyone, men did not normally get touched or raped or anything like that, did they? I had never heard of a case where a man had successfully had a woman prosecuted for raping him or even sexually assaulting him, it was normally the other way around.

The more I thought about it, the worse I felt. I had to convince everyone that me, Jeremy the Gigolo Buxton, as I was called in London, was assaulted by a woman.

Kelsey's car pulled into the drive and my heart leapt into my mouth, which had dried instantly at the thought that she would see there was something wrong. Stuart carried Harry in behind her, she sounded so excited by the thought that I was home, guilt flooded my veins and drowned my heart. How the hell was I going to be able to do this?

"Hello," she beamed and dived into my arms.

"Hello," I smiled slightly.

"This is a nice surprise," she added and pecked my lips lightly.

"Yeah, Mark said that I could have a long weekend, you know, because I had worked so late this week." I explained.

"That's brilliant," she beamed. Harry held out his arms to me.

"It is," I agreed and took Harry from Stuart's arms. "Nice to see you, mate, how are you?" I asked Stuart.

"Um, I am getting there, I suppose." He sighed. "Thank you for letting me stay, I promise, I will be out of your hair as soon as I can."

"There is no rush," I stated. "I told Kelsey you can stay as long as you want."

"I am going to put the kettle on," Kelsey announced and left the room.

"Are you alright, mate?" Stuart asked. "You look like you are about to throw up."

"I'm okay," I lied and sat on the couch with Harry on my lap.

"I know something is wrong, mate, you can't lie to me." He muttered so that Kelsey wouldn't hear.

I shook my head, "I am absolutely shattered, I have been working my arse off on signing this contract and the bitch keeps finding something wrong with it. I swear, she is just trying to make my life hell, I feel like telling them to shove it." I grumbled.

"And do what?"

"I have no idea," I frowned.

Kelsey came in with two mugs of tea. I put Harry on the floor and took a cup from her. She smiled warmly as I thanked her. She looked amazing that afternoon, the cool wind outside had put colour into her cheeks and made her blue eyes sparkle, it only made me feel worse.

After talking the afternoon away, we decided to order a take away for dinner. I didn't want to eat anything to be honest, every time I laughed at something Stuart had said or caught my wife smiling at me, my body filled with guilt and I felt sick. Natasha had the power to take all of it away from me, no matter what I did or said now, I would always look guilty.

Who would believe a man if he said that a woman forcibly masturbated him? I know I wouldn't. What was that anyway? Was it a sexual act? I suppose it was, I didn't consent to her grabbing me like that and I certainly didn't consent to her making me ejaculate, I didn't want to, she made me. The thought of it made me feel sick again. Yes she was very beautiful, but that did not give her the right to do that to me.

As we sat there I wondered what I had done to give her the impression that I would be interested in her like that. Did I lead her on? Did I give her the impression that I wanted an affair? I had everything I wanted, even though things at home had been strained, I would still take that over losing it all through no fault of my own.

After a couple of cans of larger with Stuart, I finally started to relax. Kelsey's cheeks glowed the way they always did after a couple of glasses of wine, her eyes twinkled as I stared at her from across the room, not believing that yes, though we were far from perfect, she was mine.

Stuart went to bed after another hour or so, leaving just us, everything was fine, I felt relaxed and she came to sit with me, snuggling into my body. I wrapped my arm around her and pulled her in close, then kissed the top of her head, inhaling the scent of her shampoo. She moved her face towards mine and pressed her lips to my mouth. I kissed her deeply, pushing my hand into her hair and pulling her closer to me.

Her hand began to trail down my body towards my pulsing groin, but as her hand smoothed over my erection, I pulled away from her lips. For a split second she looked like Natasha.

"Are you okay?" she asked.

"Yes," I lied. "I uh, I need the loo." I stood from the couch and hurried to the downstairs bathroom.

It took a few moments to get it together before braving the living room, when I got back to Kelsey she was reading at text on my phone.

"So, you met with Natasha today as well?" she asked.

I snatched my phone from her, "She said she would sign the contracts," I snapped, "she lied, she's a lying, manipulating bitch."

"I only…"

I looked into her eyes, "Sorry, love, she is really pissing me off." I sighed thinking I needed to put a code on my phone just in case.

"Well, maybe you should tell her that because, '*Thanks for today, Jeremy, just what I needed,*' is not the sort of message you send to someone you are pissing off."

"Maybe I should," I agreed. "Look, I am tired, are you coming to bed or not?"

"I wanted to watch a movie with my husband," she replied sourly.

"I'll watch a movie with you tomorrow night," I bent down and pecked the top of her head. She shrugged me off again, *here we go again.* "Night, love."

"Yeah," she sighed.

When I got up to my room I flicked on the light and sat on the bed,

'*Fuck off and leave me alone,*' I texted back to Natasha and switched my phone off.

Seven

Kelsey

It was all going so well, Jeremy was back to his old self, laughing and joking with Stuart about the men he thought batted for the other side in his office. Stuart offered his expertise on the matter by going to work on Monday with Jeremy as his new secretary. Jeremy suggested he shave his legs because all the secretaries at the office had great legs and he had to compete with them. I didn't let it bother me, I knew he was joking, well maybe I did, but I wouldn't let it show and ruin a really good evening.

Stuart went to bed as pissed as a hand cart shortly after eleven, leaving Jeremy on the sofa, I meandered over to him and snuggled into his body. I was horny again, I'll admit that, I wanted sex and I didn't care where we had it, I just wanted him. We kissed and when I touched him, he freaked out, if that didn't tell me that he didn't want me anymore, I didn't know what would. I let him go to bed and I stayed up watching, or rather, glaring at the TV.

After a couple of hours, I climbed between the cool sheets of my bed and rested my weary and worn out head against the pillow. I could hear him breathing, steady and deep, he was asleep and I suppose at least if he wasn't bothered by the concept of our marriage ending, maybe he was just tired. Either way, it bought me to tears, I turned away from his warm breath and cried silently as he slept beside me.

Something about the way he was acting seemed more off than usual. Okay, so he rejected me, I have sort of turned into a nympho, maybe he really was just tired. I'd believe that if he didn't seem so distant, not just that night, but most nights. I wasn't imagining the space between us in bed, that cold patch of bed that never seemed to get warm. The lonely place where I would rest my hand during the night by accident and move it quickly not wanting to believe that perhaps we weren't as strong as I thought after all. That maybe Jeremy had truly had enough. I know he denied these thoughts, but words seemed so little compared to his actions, I felt like I was losing the battle and it left me anxious and feeling desperately lonely.

I thought about the times we had parted before, when I let him go to marry Tara and then after losing our baby, how I pushed him too far then. It almost destroyed me completely and took everything I had in me to learn to trust him and my heart again. All of that appeared to be in vein now as I came to the harsh realization that Jeremy was going to leave me, that he had already decided that I was not worth the fight anymore. The emptiness flooded my world weary soul and yet he was still beside me. I wondered how I would ever cope if I lost him again, I supposed that no matter how hard you hold on to someone, if they want to go, it was out of your control.

"Get off me," Jeremy called out in the dark. I jumped awake and snapped my eyes open as he sat up beside me.

"Jeremy, what is it?" I asked as fear drowned my veins.

"A nightmare, go back to sleep," he said pushing off the covers.

"Where are you going?" I asked.

"I need a drink, just go back to sleep." He said coldly and stood from the bed before leaving the room. I felt even colder than before.

My wine drenched body had sobered and my heart felt heavy and overwhelmed. There was no compassion in his voice, it was as if I disgusted him and I didn't know what to do. More tears filled my eyes and I couldn't stop them from falling, I wanted to talk to him, have it out with him to find out what was wrong. So I pushed off the covers and pulled my robe over my body. I tiptoed through the house and found him sat at the breakfast bar in the kitchen.

Wearing only his boxers and leaning over a steaming cup of coffee, he frowned as I entered the kitchen. I could see he was cold, his lips were white and his bare arms were covered in goose bumps, he also appeared to be shaking. I removed his hoody from the back of the chair and handed it to him. He took it and pulled it over his head.

"You need to sleep," he grumbled.

"How can I sleep?" I frowned and sat beside him. He just glared at the cup. "I'm worried about you," I added bravely.

"I don't want you to worry about me," he groaned, "I'm fine."

"Yes, well you don't sound fine and you don't look fine," I countered.

"What can you do about it, eh?" he demanded.

"I want to help you," I went to place my hand on his shoulder and he moved away. My hand hovered briefly before I pulled it back and rested it on the counter.

"You can't help me, no one can. I am in this on my own."

"In what?" I asked.

He pursed his lips, "It doesn't matter, nothing matters anymore."

Pain stabbed at my heart, he seemed so detached, it petrified me, "Including me?"

"That's it," he barked, "make it all about you."

Tears pierced my already sore eyes, "I didn't…" I sniffed.

"God, you are such a bloody drama queen. You can't fix this, no one can." He growled.

"Fix what?" I frowned, "What have you done?"

He scoffed and fidgeted in his seat, "Of course you blame me, so typical." He stood from his seat, the feet of the stool scraped loudly on the floor and it made me jump. "You are suffocating me, Kelse, I can't stand it anymore." He added and left the kitchen. I just sat there unable to move, that one sentence crushed me, what the hell was I going to do?

I heard him hurry up to our room and the squeak of him sitting on the bed. I left it a few moments before going up and braving him once more. Deciding that I couldn't be near him without wanting to smash his face in, I walked in to our room and without even looking at him, I pulled the crimson throw from the chair and lifted my pillow from the bed.

"What are you doing?" he asked coldly.

"Nothing," I snapped and hurried back down stairs.

I made a bed up on the sofa and climbed in still wearing my robe, despair had turned to anger briefly, but now I just felt totally devastated.

Everything felt so out of control, out of *my* control. That was the problem, I controlled who I let in and out of my life, but it looked as though I was not going to control anything this time. Jeremy felt that I suffocated him and that would lead to a trial separation and eventually divorce, I knew all too well where this road was headed. Distance led to separation which led to a permanent end to our lives together. I saw it happen to my parents, I saw it happen everywhere I looked. I just wondered how we got to this point so quickly. He must have hated me and I didn't blame him truth be told, even I hated me at times. When Harrison was sick I became intolerable, I didn't blame Jeremy for wanting out, it just seemed so sudden.

When the pain inside hurt too much to breathe and my head felt like it would burst with pressure, I turned over and faced the back of the sofa. Jeremy thought that I suffocated him, he couldn't stand it anymore. It played over and over in my head as more tears streamed my face and soaked my pillow.

I woke a few hours later and as soon as I opened my eyes I remembered the night before. Everyone else was still asleep so I went back upstairs and took a hot shower before Harrison woke wanting his breakfast. I braved our bedroom so that I could get some clothes. I gently sat on the bed with my towel wrapped around my body and pulled open my drawer. I found my underwear I wanted and lifted my jeans and jumper from the chair. I hurried out of the room and in to Harrison. He was still sleeping which was great for me, it meant that I could get a cup of tea before he woke.

Sat at the kitchen table, I wrapped my hands around a hot cup of tea and sighed. I felt empty and useless. Hearing the bed creak upstairs made my heart leap into my mouth, he was getting up and I didn't know how I would cope seeing him, seeing his unfeeling eyes.

He stepped off the creaky, bottom stair and walked into the kitchen; he had Harrison in his arms, he silently carried him to his highchair and strapped him in. He turned and frowned slightly before opening the cabinet to get Harrison some breakfast.

"Where is his cereal?" he asked.

I cleared my strained throat, "He prefers toast at the moment," I muttered.

"Right," he nodded and pulled the toaster forward. I stood from the table leaving my cup, still filled with tea standing there and hurried up the stairs.

I got some clothes for Harrison and opened his blinds, made his bed and opened a window. I turned off the humidifier and allowed the room to breathe. I then went to our room, made the bed and opened the curtains and windows, again everything felt stuffy, suffocating.

After some composing breaths I went back down the stairs. Harrison was toddling around the living room with the television on and Jeremy was out in the kitchen. I changed Harrison and dressed him. The more mobile he had got, the harder it was to pin him down so that I could dress him. Eventually though he was and as soon as I let him go, he was off again. I took his washing out to the kitchen. Jeremy was sat at the table with a cup of black tea.

"Are you going to sulk all day?" he asked.

"I'm not sulking," I shrugged and loaded the washing machine.

"Would it help if I said I am sorry?"

"I don't think it will," I frowned.

"Well, I am."

"And it doesn't matter," I sighed and stood from the floor.

"What is that supposed to mean?" he frowned as I spun around to face him.

"Nothing matters, remember?" I snapped and turned away, counting to ten in my head so that I didn't start crying again.

"I'd had a bad dream, Kelse, I wasn't feeling too great and you kept on and on, I didn't mean it."

"What, you didn't mean that I don't matter anymore or that I suffocate you?" I turned to face him again and folded my arms over my chest.

"All of it, I was just venting,"

"What's going on?" I asked after a few moments.

"It's just work, okay? I am a bit stressed out and I took it out on you, I'm sorry."

"That's all you seem to say to me lately," I accused.

"You haven't exactly been a picnic lately either." He snapped.

I shook my head, "No, but I have never pushed you away or told you that you are suffocating me. I was worried about you, but I won't bother in future." I retorted and left him in the kitchen and almost bumping into Stuart.

I hurried up the stairs and picked up my phone, I pressed Jude's number, praying she was there, it only rang a couple of times before she answered,

"You had better have a good reason for calling this early on a Saturday." She groaned.

I looked at the clock, it was only just nine, "Sorry, I'll call back." I muttered as tears pierced my eyes.

"I'm awake now, what's up?"

"Everything," I sniffed.

"Are you crying, is Harry okay?"

I didn't even bother to correct her, they all called him Harry. "Yes, he's fine, its uh, its, look, are you busy this morning?"

"I was going to have a lie in, but we can meet in Poole if you want."

"That would be perfect," I sniffed again. "Thank you."

"It's alright, give me an hour and I'll meet you in Starbucks, okay?"

"I'll see you there." I nodded and ended the call. I then straightened my hair and put on a little make up to at least look alive and happy even if I didn't feel it.

As I came down the stairs Stuart greeted me in the hall,

"Your mum called, she is coming to take Harrison out to see your aunt, Jez said it was alright."

"Oh, okay."

"I'm meeting Shawna and Nicki in Bournemouth, Felix might be able to get me a job at the Golf club he works at now, apparently they are looking for someone in admin. So, you two can have some much needed time alone," he winked and nudged me playfully.

"I'm meeting someone," I replied. "I have plans."

"Can't you postpone them?" he asked.

"No," I answered.

"So, you are going to leave him here alone?"

"Yes, it will give him some of that space he seems to crave lately." I retorted sourly.

"I thought you wanted to get back on track." He whispered.

"I did, right up until I was made to feel that I wasn't welcome in my own bed last night." I muttered. "I have to hurry or I'll be late."

"Fine," he sighed and ran up the stairs.

I walked out to the kitchen, Jeremy was washing up, "I have to meet Jude in town. Mum's on her way over; can you make sure Harrison has nappies and some snacks in the bag?"

"Why are you meeting Jude?" he frowned.

"We are going to talk about the wedding," I lied.

"So you've made up then?" he checked.

"Yes, I am going to be late." I said lifting my handbag. Harrison grabbed hold of my legs, I lifted him up and kissed his cheek. "Be good for Nannie, okay?"

"Okay," he promised and it melted me a little. I kissed him again and handed him to Jeremy.

"What time will you be back?" he asked.

"I don't know yet," I replied coolly, "enjoy your day."

"I wanted to spend the day with my family," he grumbled.

"Mmm, but wasn't that before you told me I suffocate you?"

He sighed loudly, "You are not going to let it go, are you?"

"Not any time soon, no." I answered and left him in the kitchen. I grabbed my keys from the unit in the hall and hurried out to my car before I changed my mind.

I sat with a latte while I waited almost another hour for Jude to arrive. I should have learned by now that she is not the best time keeper in the world, but still, I got to enjoy a coffee in peace and watch the world pass by. Just as I was preparing to text her, she burst through the door, though I hardly recognised her with brown hair. She looked amazing, I loved her red hair, don't get me wrong, but when she reverted back to her normal colour, it took me to memories of a better time in my life.

"Bloody traffic," she grumbled. "I need a wee."

"You go to the loo, I'll get us some coffee."

"Fab," she beamed and hurried through the shop. After waiting in the que for ten minutes, she emerged and came and stood with me. I ordered two lattes and before I could pay, she placed a ten pound note on the counter. "These are on me," she said.

"Thank you," I smiled politely and when our drinks were ready we headed back to the table.

"So, what's up?" she asked as we sat down.

"I'd rather talk about your wedding," I insisted.

"No, you look like you've had your face slapped, Kelse, what's happened?"

I thought for a few moments, staring at the froth on my coffee as the tiny bubbles popped, I didn't want to tell her that my husband didn't want to have sex with me anymore, that he was sick of me, but I knew Jude, "Its Jeremy," I said thinly, "something is wrong and I don't know what to do."

"What do you mean, wrong?"

"Well, he's distant, staying out all hours, going to work early and coming home late. When I try to show him affection he is standoffish and I don't know what I have done wrong."

"Other than being a first class B.I.T.C.H. Seriously, mate, you have a degree in it."

"Okay, I have been a bit stressed." I admit.

"A bit?" she scoffed. "Babes, you have been a complete and utter bitch to him for over two years. The bloke is only human and I am surprised you haven't realized it yet." I frowned, "Oh, come on, don't act all innocent, Kelsey Buxton, you know I am telling the truth."

"Okay, so I am to blame, I get it." I sighed and sat back in my seat.

"Don't be a victim, Kelse, do something about it."

"If he won't talk to me about it, how can I do anything about it?" I frowned, I thought seeing Jude would help. She made me feel worse, but more than that, she made me feel responsible.

"Talk to him, even when you think he is not listening, talk till you are blue in the face. He'll go crazy listening to you rant on and on and then he'll tell you. The Buxton boys have been raised to deal with their shit on their own, not to talk about your problems with anyone, much less a sodding girl. It's not his fault, it's the way his father has made him."

"So, it's my fault and his dad's fault that he has rejected me and pushed me away. It's his dad's fault that he doesn't talk to me or has nightmares, you know what, lets change the subject, if he has given up on us, there is nothing I can do to change that." I spat and pushed my coffee away.

Eight

Jeremy

"What's going on with you two?" Stuart asked as he stepped in from the kitchen. I lifted Harry to put on his shoes ready for Kelsey's mum.

"We had words," I shrugged.

"Words, mmm, so the cold and frosty vibes I am getting from you two, it's nothing, right?"

"Okay, I didn't want to have drunk sex with her last night on the sofa and now she is pissed off at me for it." I snapped and put Harry on the floor, he turned around and gave me a stern grimace, "Sorry, mate," I said and ruffled his hair as the door-bell echoed out through the house.

"Nannie!" Harry announced and ran out to the hall after Stuart. I lifted his bag and prayed that she'd be alright with me, after all, I seemed to be pissing everyone off.

The older version of my wife stepped into the living room closely followed by Dave, "Hello, Jeremy," she smiled warmly and pecked my cheek. "Where's Kelsey?"

"She had to meet Jude in Poole, wedding planning I think." I replied. "Are you sure you want to take Harry out?" I asked.

"If I am going to look after him while Kelsey works, then he'll have to get used to being with us more," she explained. "Are you alright, you look tired?"

"I am tired, work is getting me down at the moment too." I lied. "So, you are really going to look after him for us?" I checked, I didn't know it had been finalised.

"Yes," she nodded. "So, it's just work then?"

"Yes, we have a big contract coming in and it's been hectic." I explained. I was not going to admit to my mother-in-law that I had upset her daughter so much that she felt she couldn't share a room with me, let alone the same bed.

"Kelsey said you have been working a lot of overtime, I hope they pay you for it," she added.

"They said they will," I lied again, shit, this was getting too easy.

"Nannie, go." Harrison moaned.

"We'd better go," she smiled slightly. Dave and I will bring him back around five, is that alright with you?"

"Sure that's great, thank you, Jane." I smiled slightly, it actually hurt my face.

"It's alright, you go back to bed and get some rest." She said as she lifted Harry's bag. I lifted Harry and kissed his cheek.

"You be a good boy, okay?" I said as I kissed him once more.

"Okay," he smiled. I couldn't believe he was actually mine.

He amazed me the more he grew. I watched them leave and I couldn't help feeling the sense of loss. I was on my way to losing him, losing everything and that's when panic set in.

"Jez, tell me what's going on, mate," Stuart frowned. "Why are you sleeping apart and why is she in tears every time I try and talk to her?"

"Because I am an arsehole, that's why."

"You're hot headed and stubborn, but I wouldn't say you were an arsehole, trust me, I know a lot of arseholes and you don't come close to any of them."

"Are you positive about that?" I checked. "Sit down, I am sure I can change your mind." I added and sat on the chair. Stuart sat on the couch and frowned. "I have had a lot of dinner meetings recently trying to sign this bitch from London with a load of celeb mags under her belt. Her name is Natasha Mason, she is worth billions and will really boost the company. I have written the contracts, but she has found something wrong with them three times now, so I have done them over and over again. I found out yesterday it's because she wanted to see me."

"See you?"

"Yes, as in 'let's have an affair', *I want you to fuck me and if you don't, I am telling your wife you did anyway, you lose no matter what you do.*"

"No, way!"

"Yes, and on top of that she has these pictures of me with women, before Kelsey, or when we were apart, anyway, in the pictures I am drunk off my face and having sex with these other women, whom I don't even remember and now Natasha's blackmailing me, threatening my job and my life just so that I will sleep with her." I admitted.

"You have to tell Kelsey, if you are completely innocent, mate, she'll believe you." I felt the little colour I had in my cheeks drain away like someone had pulled a plug of the back of my head. "Jez, you, you haven't, have you?"

"God, no, no way."

"But something happened," he pressed, the room felt so small all of a sudden, I stood from the sofa, he would see this as bad, of course he would. "Did you kiss her?"

"No," I frowned.

"Grab a little boob action? I know how you like boobs." He smiled.

I frowned and swallowed, "Who told you that?"

"Seb," he shrugged. "Jez, tell me." He pressed.

"I didn't touch her, I swear."

He thought for a few moments, "So, she touched you?" I couldn't move, I just stood there, "She did, didn't she?"

"Yes, we were sat in my car and before she got out, she grabbed me and started rubbing and I tried to fight it, I tried, but… it happened. I didn't want to cum for her, I didn't want to give that to her, but I did and now she is texting me and calling me hourly. I turned my phone off so Kelsey doesn't find out." I sat on the chair. "Kelsey will see this as cheating, she would say that she must have turned me on, which she didn't and…"

"So, she grabbed your dick and tossed you off without your consent?"

"Yes, I mean, no. I told her to stop, I tried to push her off and then it was over, too late. I threw her out of my car and came home." The humiliation crippled me, just admitting it out loud crushed all of my pride.

"What a dirty, little bitch." He sighed.

"You can't tell anyone, Stuart. I will sort it out, just don't tell Kelsey or anyone else." I pleaded.

"But she sexually assaulted you," he frowned.

"And I came, so…"

"You're a man, you have no control over these things, did you enjoy it?"

I shook my head, "No, actually it hurt."

"You need to tell the police, cover your own arse and please, whatever you do, do not meet with her alone again." His phone pinged in his pocket, "I have to go, look, if she tries to contact you again, let me know, alright?"

"You can't tell anyone, Stuart, I'm ashamed by what she did to me, no one would believe me anyway." I shrugged.

"I do," he said placing his hand on my leg. I looked down at his hand, he removed it quickly, "Don't worry, sunshine, you are not my type." He smirked.

"That's actually good to know," I nodded.

He left shortly after and I began working on a few contracts in my office. I suppose you could say I felt a little better after talking to Stuart, but it didn't change the fact that some psycho, bunny boiler was trying to ruin my life. I texted Kelsey just before eleven in the hope that she would respond, but she didn't and I guess she had a few good reasons not to. I couldn't help what I said, I opened my mouth and words seemed to fall out.

I had never felt that she suffocated me, not until that night when she put me on the spot. She had backed me into a corner and it wasn't even her fault. In retaliation for that, I hit back with something that wasn't true, at least I didn't think it was. The hurt registered immediately on her face and now I feared that the damage had been done. Kelsey never forgot a thing, this would come back to bite me on the arse every time we had words from now on, she would use that one sentence.

I tried to eat a sandwich at lunch time, the truth is though, I couldn't swallow, the stress and anxiety I felt prevented me from forcing the bread down my throat. After only a bite, I threw it away. I washed up my plate and made sure the house looked tidy. The cool breeze from upstairs made the bottom half of the house feel so cold, so I ran up to close the windows Kelsey insisted on opening every weekend to air the house through.

As I got to our window, I caught a glimpse of a silver sports style Mercedes parked across from our drive. I recognized the car immediately, she looked up at me and smiled, my heart began to race in my chest as my phone rang in my pocket. I forgot to turn it back off again, twat!

"Hello handsome," Natasha chimed.

"How did you find my house?" I demanded.

"I have my resources," she answered. "Aren't you going to invite me in?"

"Can't you take a hint? Fuck off!" I snapped angrily and ended the call.

I hurried down the stairs as the doorbell echoed out in the empty house, I pulled open the door, she smiled warmly. "I only wanted to talk, to offer you a deal."

"Fine," I frowned, "you'd better come in then." I allowed her to step inside, her perfume was so strong it burned my throat.

"This is nice, it's so… you." She grinned. She removed her coat from her shoulders, dropping it on the floor. Her cream dress scooped revealing her flawless back. Her peach skin appeared soft and just below her right shoulder blade she had a read birthmark in the shape of finger print.

"I am not picking that up," I remarked. She looked over her shoulder at me, smiled and bent over to pick it up. Her dress lifted slightly and I couldn't miss the firm curves of her backside, wondering if she actually had any underwear on at all. She placed her coat on the chair in the hall and turned to face me.

"So, are we having a coffee or do you have something stronger?" she asked.

"I am not making you welcome, you are not and never will be welcome in my home." I snapped. "What did you want to talk about?"

"I think we both could use a drink," she sighed.

"Fine, I'll make you a cup of instant coffee, then you can tell me what you have to tell me and then you can leave." I marched towards the kitchen, she followed.

"Mind if I sit down?" she asked.

"Why not," I shrugged and filled the kettle. Kelsey filters our water because the water in Poole is shit, but she could have it out of the tap, chemicals and all.

She pulled a chair out and sat, I turned to face her and folded my arms across my chest leaning back against the kitchen counter. My hands were shaking, not through fear, once more, I shook with anger. "You look tired," she muttered.

"Well, I slept like a baby, so I don't why I look tired. Mind you, it could be from making mad, passionate love to my wife most of the night though, she is such a minx." I smirked. Her face hardened, like she had sucked on a lemon and it gave me huge satisfaction to see that hearing that I had sex with my wife upset her.

I made her a cup of coffee from the cheap instant crap I picked up by accident one night in a rush to get home, it smelled terrible as I placed the cup in front of her, "Milk?" I asked.

"No, black is fine," she replied. "Thank you, Jeremy." She lifted the cup and I revelled in her face as she sipped the bitter coffee. "So, where is the little wife?" she asked after forcing it down her neck.

"Shopping and wedding planning," I answered bemused by her sour looking face. "She'll be home soon."

"Have you told her anything yet?" she asked placing the cup down, I noticed the red lipstick mark and made a mental note to make sure I washed up properly.

"No, not yet," I frowned and folded my arms over my chest again.

"I have to go back to London for a few days, so I have decided to give you a stay of execution."

"Why not just go back to London and stay there? There is nothing here for you, Natasha, there never was." I retorted.

"I don't give up that easily," she smirked.

"Neither do I. See, I am a Catholic man, I made vows to my wife and I intend to stick to them, till death us do part."

"You don't come across as the religious type?"

"At first you didn't come across as a psycho, bunny boiler, I suppose we were both wrong." My phone began to ring in my pocket, I pulled it out, it was Kelsey. I answered with a smile, "Hello my love, are you okay?"

"Um, yeah, sorry I didn't get your message till now. I just wanted to make sure Mum picked Harrison up okay."

"Yeah, he couldn't wait to go. How is Jude? Excited about the wedding I bet."

"She is," I could tell Kelsey was confused. "Look, about this morning…"

"Its fine, we'll make up for it later," I grinned.

"Okay, I'll see you about four."

"Great, can't wait, I love you," I stated.

"Love you too," she muttered and ended the call. I knew it had thrown her off, and I knew I shouldn't have used her like that, but the look on Natasha's face was so worth it. "Sorry, where were we?"

"I should go," she stood from the table. "Just remember, all I want is to wrap these long legs around your waist and fuck you till Kingdom come." She smiled.

"Just remember that I am a happily, married man and you'll be waiting until Poole harbour freezes over." I retorted. "And just so you know, that has never happened, so you might want to rethink your plan."

She stared and sighed loudly, "Like I said, I don't give up that easily. I always get what I want." She retorted. We stood silent for a few moments. "Can I use your bathroom before I go?" she asked.

"Yes," I frowned and walked towards the hall, I pulled open the downstairs bathroom door, she looked disappointed. "You didn't think I'd let you go upstairs, did you?"

"Of course not," she shrugged and stepped into the bathroom.

I hurried back to the kitchen and put her coffee cup in the sink. She was in there a while, when I went to knock on the door, she appeared in front of me.

"Thank you for the coffee," she said and lifted her coat from the chair. She pulled it over her shoulders and walked towards the door. "I'll be in touch."

I didn't respond and happily watched as she left. I closed the door and locked it behind her. Her stink was everywhere; I didn't realize it until after she had gone. The house stank of her, I opened the French doors and the back door to try and eradicate the overwhelmingly, sweet perfume that seemed to fill the house.

I washed up her cup up carefully making sure I removed very last trace of her lipstick mark she had left on the side of it. I sprayed a little air freshener around until I had eradicated every trace of her from the house, or so I thought.

I heard Kelsey's car on the drive, stood from the sofa and switched off the TV. I felt nervous, I guess from the stink Natalie had left in the house she could tell that another woman had been there. I hadn't done anything wrong, but I already felt I was misplacing her trust.

She came through the living room door and smile sheepishly. I jammed my shaking and sweaty hands into my jean pockets.

"You cleaned up," she said.

"I was bored," I shrugged.

"What's that smell?" she frowned sniffing the air. "It's nice." She added placing her bags on the floor.

"Oh, uh, had a sample of a uh, a new air freshener, it's a Fabreeze one or something. I went a bit overboard with it," I lied to my wife - *I LIED TO MY WIFE!* - What a bloody idiot?

"So, what was it called?" she asked.

"I don't remember it now, I'll know it when I see it." *Stop lying, idiot!*

"Smell's expensive," she shrugged. "So, uh, about that phone call, was everything alright?"

"After you had all gone I realised what a prat I have been lately and that I am so lucky to have you and Harry-son. I had a dream about my mother last night, I keep having them and they upset me because she is dead and reaching out for me, so…" More lies, I was fighting Natasha off, not my dead mother, *God, forgive me!*

"Oh, I thought, that it might have been about me… you seemed so distant, I suppose I am afraid of losing you." She explained. I reached out to her and took hold of her hand.

"You will never lose me, no matter what happens to us, I will always love you, Kelsey Buxton."

She pulled me into her arms and pressed her lips to mine. I warmed in her arms, melting against her body. I thought about Stuart's words and as I pulled back from her, I gazed into her amazing blue eyes.

"We still have a couple of hours before your mum brings Harry back," I grinned.

"So, what would you like to do?" she asked coyly looking up at me through her long eyelashes.

"I would like to take my wife up to our room and make love to her all afternoon long."

She grinned and her eyes twinkled, "What are we waiting for then?" she took my hand and led me up the stairs.

Nine

Kelsey

Afternoon sex to me was the best sex you could have. There is something about the fact that you could and should be doing something else, but there was nothing better than making love in the afternoon to the most amazing man in the world.

Driving home from meeting Jude I thought about how much I could lose if I continued on this road. My temper and my stubbornness could be the end of us if I allowed it. I fought too long and too hard to get the man of my dreams, Jeremy was my first and he would be my last lover. I had to take control of this situation, I would not give up without a fight.

The phone call had thrown me, I expected him to be angry or at least still pissed off with me, but he sounded happy to hear from me and that made me more determined to make sure that he knew how much I still loved and needed him in my life.

I led him up the stairs to our room with amazing scent around us, I climbed onto the bed in my underwear and allowed him to slowly and sumptuously seduce me. Kissing every inch of my body, driving me wild with ecstasy, when we came together, I saw stars, it was that amazing and so needed, I actually saw stars.

We must have fallen asleep after as my eyes snapped open at the sound of our doorbell ringing out. Jeremy pushed off the covers and pulled his jeans up his legs,

"Your mum is back." He announced.

"Great," I frowned.

"It's alright, I'll go." He affirmed as he slipped his hoodie over his head. I had never seen him dress so quickly. He hurried down the stairs and I heard the door open, "Hello, Jane, sorry, I dozed off on the couch."

"I thought you looked tired," she remarked.

"Has he been okay?"

"A little angel, Dave is bringing him in, he fell asleep in the car on the way back. Diane said to say hello, by the way, and that she hasn't seen you or Kelsey in months."

"I know, I have been so busy at work, maybe we'll pop out and see her next weekend."

"She'd like that." Mum then went on to list everything Harrison had eaten that day, including far too many white chocolate buttons. "Where is Kelsey?"

"She is shattered, she didn't sleep very well last night," he wasn't lying there.

"Where shall I put this heavy lump?" Dave asked.

"On the sofa, Dave, cheers, mate."

"He's been so good, did Jane tell you?"

"She did, thank you both for looking after him."

"It's our pleasure, love," Mum said.

"I'll put the kettle on, would you like a cuppa?"

"No ta, love, we're going out tonight, meeting Jim and Mary for a meal. So we best be off." She replied.

"Okay, thanks again."

"Don't mention it, give Kelsey our love and tell her to ring me tomorrow." Mum said before the front door closed.

It was a little while before I heard the creaky step on the stairs. Jeremy came in with a mug of steaming tea. He sat on the bed and smiled before he started singing to the tune of Cecilia,

"*Making love in the afternoon with my wife, up in our bedroom...*"

"Wow, you can sing," I smiled, "maybe you should try out for the X-Factor or something."

"Uh… no," he said lifting my hand from the bed and pressing his soft lips to the back of my hand. "I love you," he muttered.

"I love you too," I affirmed. He looked like he had something to tell me, "What is it?" I asked.

He thought for a few moments, "Nothing, well, I feel bad about last night, but…" Harrison started crying, "Drink your tea, love, I'll go and sort him out."

"I was going to take a shower," I said sitting up.

He smiled at the falling sheet as it exposed my breasts. "I'd like to join you, but…"

"Maybe we can take a bath together later." I suggested seductively.

"Not with Stuart here we can't," he stood and walked to the door, "but, if he goes out tomorrow, it's a date."

I took a shower and dressed before heading down the stairs. Blissfully happy and contented, but also dying for the loo. I hurried into the downstairs bathroom, that air freshener still lingered, but I put it down to the fact that we kept that door closed and it held the scent in the room.

We made dinner together while Harrison played with his toys, life felt normal for a change and I wasn't sure if I was being naïve that nothing could touch us. I believed it for a few moments, but then I would catch him thinking about something and his face would fill with guilt. I didn't want to think that he was hiding things from me. Surely, after all we had been through, we deserved to just be happy.

Stuart arrived home and we sat around the dining table eating and talking the evening away. While I put Harrison to bed, Jeremy and Stuart cleared the table and made coffee. I kissed Harrison goodnight and left him in his room. As I came down the stairs I could hear Jeremy and Stuart talking,

"Are you bloody stupid?" Stuart asked.

"What could I do?" Jeremy demanded.

"You are going to have to tell Kelsey," Stuart stated as I approached the kitchen.

Jeremy was rinsing the plates off under a running tap and handing them to Stuart who was stacking them in the dishwasher, "Yeah, because she…"

"Tell me what?" I frowned.

"Uh, we might have a visitor for a few weeks," he frowned and looked at Stuart, "another one."

"Who?"

"Julian, he's been playing up a bit and my father asked if I could keep an eye on him." he explained. "I said I'd ask you."

"You don't have to ask me, he's your brother." I shrugged.

"But he smokes and he's a little sod at the moment, do we really need that sort of stress?" he frowned.

I thought for a few moments, I must admit, I didn't like the idea of Julian in the house if he was smoking, "I'll let you decide, love." I am not stupid, I am not going to pretend that I didn't notice the tension between Jeremy and Stuart and I was almost certain that Julian had no intention of coming to stay, but I also knew Jeremy would never keep something important from me, I trusted him implicitly and I had no reason not to.

Over the next few days things at home improved. Jeremy and I were back to our old selves. He called me two or three times a day and texted me almost every hour. Stuart started work for a web design company in Bournemouth after Felix's company couldn't take him on. He promised he would move out as soon as he had the deposit for a flat, at that moment in time, I didn't want him to go anywhere.

I returned to work a few days later. I had to be at the office early so that Sue and I could chat before I got back into to it. It was nice to be Kelsey again, not just mummy or Jeremy's wife, Kelsey, on the end of the phone and ready to help. Sue met me in reception and led me up to the office, apologising for the delay, but in truth, I liked the extra two days at home with Harrison. I spent the first morning listening in to calls and all I could think about was if Harrison was alright with Mum and Dave.

I could see Shawna, Lou and Nicki on the other side of the office. I knew I wouldn't be working with them, they were all still on full-time contracts and I was so pleased when they came over to me in the chill out area while I sipped a cup of machine coffee.

"Hello, stranger," Shawna smiled and sat beside me.

"You know where I live," I retorted.

"I know," she smiled. "So, how are things?"

"Good, better, I think."

"Great, so glad Stuart is back too." She nodded.

"Me too," I agreed.

"It's good to have you back," Lou gleamed and hugged me.

"It feels weird, but I am sure I will get used to it." I smiled. Nicki looked a little awkward. Shawna went to get a coffee and Lou said she was going up to the canteen. "Are you alright?"

"Yes," she nodded, "I just feel a bitch after what happened at Jude's party."

"I was a mess, Nicki, I have been selfish and a terrible friend, the fact that you are even talking to me is more than I can hope for."

"You are my best friend, Kelsey, I have missed you so much." Her eyes welled with tears. "I wish I could make Harrison better for you, what you face on a daily basis must break your heart."

"I am lucky I have so many amazing friends and a wonderful husband, I see that now."

She hugged me and pecked my cheek, "I'm the lucky one." She muttered. "I have to get back, please tell me you are coming to Jude and Seb's party."

"She did mention it, I didn't think it was all confirmed yet," I frowned.

"Oh, well, it is now though she hasn't really invited anyone yet, it's a Halloween come engagement party at the Manor."

I felt a little put out, but also excited, we hadn't had a night out in months, "I know, she said she wanted it as fancy dress."

"I talked her out of that one," she smiled.

"Thank you, I didn't like the idea of having to dress up, even if I know how much it would upset Seb's parents. If we get an invite, we will be there," I promised.

"Fab," she smiled, "I'll call you later." I nodded

The afternoon flew by and I didn't realize how much I enjoyed it. Walking out of the office at two knowing my friends still had at least three hours of work left felt amazing.

Mum made me a cup of tea and then I took Harrison home. He was very tired and grizzly, I suppose he had missed me, but I had to do this. I needed to be part of what I call the real world again. Being at home was fine, but I felt out of the loop on so many things. Being back meant that I could see my friends' every day again and I liked the idea of that.

When Jeremy got home he was a little quiet and he looked tired, it seemed the day for grumpy Buxtons, I knew that much. I made dinner and bathed Harrison before putting him to bed early, then as I came back down the stairs I could hear that Stuart was home and he wasn't alone.

"Kelsey," Stuart smiled, he was sat on the sofa with an extremely good looking, dark haired man of about twenty five. His light blue eyes were edged in long dark eyelashes and he had a mouth full of perfect white teeth. "This is Elliot Robinson, he is a programmer at work."

"Hello," I said.

"Nice to uh," he sat forward and held out his hand, "nice to meet you." He smiled.

I shook his clammy hand and smiled, "We're going out for a drink, I just had to take a quick shower." Stuart said standing. "I won't be long."

"I'll make some tea," I said. "Would you both like a cup?" I asked.

"Not for me," Jeremy sighed.

"I would love one," Elliot said and stood from the sofa, "I'll help you." He followed me out to the kitchen. "So, uh, how long have you known Stuart?" he asked as I filled the kettle.

"Um, a couple of years now," I answered

"He is a nice guy," he nodded.

"Stuart is the best friend anyone could ever have. He is honest and loyal and I trust him implicitly." I smiled.

He smiled also, his face glowed, "I can't believe no one has snapped him up."

I stopped preparing the cups and turned to him, "He's just come out of a relationship."

"I know, we talked about it, we're just friends, but you never know, right?"

"Right," I smiled slightly, "he's a lovely bloke and didn't deserve what Luke did to him, so if you are prepared to wait, I am sure he will be worth it."

"I'll wait," he nodded.

After their tea they left to go to the pub just down the road from where we lived. Jeremy sighed loudly as I sat beside him on the sofa, I think he as sulking because they didn't ask him to go out with them.

"Why don't you go and see Seb for a few hours," I suggested.

"I have work tomorrow," he grumbled.

"I just thought that…"

"I'm knackered, love, I just want an early night to be honest with you."

"Sounds like a plan," I said and stood from the sofa. I held out my hand, "Come on, bed time." He stood and took my hand and we walked up the stairs together.

We got in to bed and I kissed him goodnight, he smiled slightly, I honestly think he thought I wanted to have sex, I would have, but I knew how much he needed to sleep and I was just as tired. I switched off the light and cuddled into my husband before falling into a deep and blissful sleep.

Ten

Jeremy

Bullshit had become my new second language. It literally fell out of my mouth whenever Kelsey asked me anything I didn't want her knowing the truth about. It started with the stupid air freshener lie I told her to cover up Natasha's sickly, sweet perfume that had filled the house when she visited. I said the first thing to come to my mind and I knew it would come back to bight me on the arse and soon.

Yes, Natasha had gone back to London and for the first few days I felt great. Kelsey and I were getting along well and I enjoyed our afternoon of making love before Harrison came back that Saturday. As the week passed by it felt like a ticking clock was hovering above me and as the hours wound down to my imminent doom, the bell began to toll.

I couldn't even concentrate at work and missed so many typos in an important contact, if it hadn't have been for Sian, I could have ended up in Mark's office. That Tuesday lunch time I snapped at two of my colleagues, Reece and Martin, over something I took completely the wrong way, actually, no I didn't take it the wrong way at all. They both knew what they were saying and if it hadn't have been for Seb, I would have smacked them both in the mouth.

I walked past them in the corridor just outside of the office, Martin, a short red haired bloke with what could only be described as a vagina growing on his face, snickered at something Reece, a tall and skinny, blond kid, straight out of Uni, had said. With my hackles already on edge and knackered from no sleep the night before, I turned on my heels and faced them both,

"Do you have something to say?" I asked.

"Not really," Martin smirked.

I looked at Reece, "Well?"

"Something was said about you and Miss Mason," Reece shrugged.

"Oh yeah," I frowned and folded my arms over my chest, "like what?"

"Like, how she commented on how roomy your car is the other day, especially in the back." He answered.

"How would she know how roomy my car is?" I asked.

"You were seen on Friday," Martin explained. "After Mark had asked you to go on some errands for him, she was in your car with you in the car park of the Crown."

"She asked me to drop by because she had something for me," I lied.

"And we all heard what she had for you, red lace knickers and cherry flavoured ribbed condoms" Martin grinned. "It's alright, mate, no one will tell your misses, your secret is safe with us."

"There is no fucking secret you halfwit, I can't stand the bitch and I can assure you on my bollocks, there were no lacy knickers or condoms in sight."

"Well, I heard she had you right in the palm of her hand, figuratively speaking of course." He grinned. I moved towards him, Reece placed his hand on my heaving chest.

"Mate, calm down," Reece warned.

"Nothing happened, why can't you get that through your thick head?" I growled through my teeth.

"If nothing happened, why are you acting so defensively?" Martin retorted. I charged again.

"Hey, hey, hey," Seb called and pulled me back, "what's going on?"

"Seems like Mark's golden boy is fucking up, literally," Martin snapped.

"Jez?"

"They are full of shit," I barked and walked out of the building, slamming the door behind me. If they had heard something, it would get back to Kelsey, my marriage was coming to an end and I had no control over anything anymore including my temper.

"Jeremy," Seb called out chasing me across the car park. "Jeremy, wait." I stopped walking and turned to him. "What's going on?" he asked.

"Nothing," I lied.

"Bollocks, I have never seen you this upset. Not even when we had that fight over Kelsey." He pressed.

"I uh… I… I can't tell you, Seb, you are shit at keeping secrets."

"Thank you very much," he groaned.

"You know I am right." I reasoned.

"Well, I am betting it has something to do with that Natasha bird and if the rumours are true, then you deserve everything that's coming your way." He snapped.

"That's exactly what everyone will think whether its true or not, so why should you be any different?" I retorted angrily.

"I have always backed you up, when you fought with your old man, when you had nowhere to go, I stood by you, but if you are fucking that whore behind Kelsey's back then, well, you are no cousin of mine."

"I am not fucking anyone but my wife," I barked. "She is all I want, who I love, so why would I throw that away over a two bit tart from London?"

"So the rumours are?"

"Complete and utter bollocks," I affirmed. "Come on, Seb, I am a one girl man, you know that."

"You had two on the go once before, so…"

"I was nineteen and she had left the country, so I wasn't technically cheating," I shrugged.

He stared at me then nodded his head. "Okay, so what's going on then?"

I took him to my car and I told him everything, showed him the messages she had sent me and what I had sent back. He heaved a sigh and let it out slowly, misting up my windscreen briefly.

"Right, so what you have here then is a fucking psycho." He said handing my phone back to me. "If you let this escalate then you will lose everything, Jez. You need to take charge, tell her to fuck off and never speak or see her again."

"She knows where I live, for all I know, she could be there now."

"You have to tell your wife, Jez, she needs to know."

"Kelsey won't believe me, Seb, she won't. You know more than anyone what she's like." I sighed, emotion pinched at my eyes, this bitch was wrecking my life and I didn't know what to do.

"Come on, mate, she will listen, show her the messages, show it all to her and take the power away from Natasha." I nodded and blinked as a tear dripped and splashed on my hand. He placed his hand on my shoulder and squeezed it lightly. "It will be alright."

I nodded and sniffed back my tears, "Yes, it will," I stated. I knew one thing, I had to man up, Seb was right. I needed to take control of this and not allow her to destroy my life.

"Go home and talk to her now, if you tell her and she gets angry, call me and I'll talk to her. She'll fly off the handle knowing her, but she'll calm down and then Natasha has nothing on you."

"What about my job? If I don't sleep with her she will not sign the contracts, Mark will…"

"Back you up one hundred percent. You need to worry about your marriage first." He opened the door, "Let me know how it goes." He climbed out of the car. I could see Sian racing over to my car.

"Jeremy," she yelled running up to us, "Sorry," she added breathlessly. "Mark needs to see you."

"I was just going home," I frowned.

"You can't, everything is buggered up, Mark is freaking out in there." I climbed out of my car and hurried in to the office. Passing Martin and Reece in the corridor, I followed Sian to Mark's office.

"Thank God!" He proclaimed as I entered. "Tell me you have your car here." He said.

"Yes," I nodded.

"Great," he put on his jacket. "We are driving to London."

"What?" I frowned and looked as Seb, "I can't, I…"

"I need you, Jeremy, no one else knows how to set up the Ulysses system. It's crashed at head office and they can't print anything until we go and sort it out. I'll pay you double plus a bonus for taking us. Please, mate, I am desperate. My arse is on the line here."

"Jez, you need to talk to Kelsey." Seb insisted.

"How long will we be up there?" I asked.

"A few hours, possibly a night in a Travelodge, then we'll drive right back tomorrow."

"And we won't be meeting up with the Mason's or anything?" I checked.

"No, they are out of the country, some important meeting in New York. We'll go to head office and that's it."

"I need to call Kelsey." I stated.

"Great, suppose I had better phone my other half too." He nodded.

I followed Seb out of the room, "You need your bloody head testing," he snapped.

"If I do this, I might be able to talk to Mark about it, he'll see my side of it, he has to understand."

"I doubt that," Seb smirked. "Do you know who he is married to?"

"No," I shook my head.

"His husband is called Steven and he is a company director at a huge employment agency in Bournemouth. They have been married a year, you didn't know he was gay?"

"Obviously not," I sighed.

"I thought you knew," he frowned. "So, how do you convince a gay man to be on your side against a narcissistic psycho, he would never understand." He sighed. "I think we need to set a trap for the bitch, make a plan and be one step ahead of her, but first you need to tell Kelsey everything. Still, it's your life and if it does put you in favour of the boss, at least you'll still have a job when your wife kicks you out."

"Seb…" I began, he raised his hand and walked away. He had a point, but what could I do?

Kelsey answered after one ring, she had been a little frosty for a few days and I knew this would not help matters.

"What are you doing Friday night?" I asked.

"Nothing," she replied.

"You are now, we are going out." I stated.

"We'll need a babysitter."

"We have one, he lives with us." I smiled slightly. "We're going out and I am spoiling you rotten, but there is a condition."

"There always is," she sighed. "Come on then, out with it."

"I have to go to London."

"When?" she asked.

"Now, Mark needs me to drive him up to Head Office, there has been a major crash of the printing system, we need to go and fix it."

"That's what I.T. guys are for," she retorted.

"I know, sweetheart. I'm sorry, but it might mean some extra money." I reasoned.

"Doesn't sound like I have much choice, does it?" she sighed.

"Sorry," I frowned.

"I know. When will you be back?"

"Tomorrow afternoon at the latest. It's going to take us a good few hours to get there." I explained, "Mark has mentioned a Travelodge. I will make this up to you, I promise."

"Oh, I know you will, starting with a full body massage, followed by hours of endless love making and that's just to start with."

"I am sure I can arrange that," I smiled. "I love you."

"I love you too, just call me when you get there."

"I will, kisses to you and Harry."

"Kisses to you too, babe," she replied. I put my phone back into my pocket and waited for Mark to come out of his office.

"Jeremy," Martin said cautiously, "about earlier, it was just a bit of fun, you're a stand up bloke and we shouldn't have ripped the piss out of you, it's obviously a very upsetting thing to go through."

"Well, normally I wouldn't have minded, but that sort of stuff could end my marriage and if you think I am a grumpy bastard now, imagine that a thousand times worse if my misses finds out what you are all saying about me."

"Maybe you need to stop Miss Mason sending us emails with details if it's not true." Reece suggested.

"Do me a favour, either forward them to me or print them all off and keep them for when I get back. I might need them and if you hear anything else from her, do not let on you have told me."

"Sure, mate, no probs," Martin shrugged and left me standing outside of Mark's office.

He finally emerged still talking on the phone to his husband. I had no idea. I mean, I thought Stuart was Kelsey's new boyfriend once, so it seemed I was clueless at this sort of thing. I tried not to listen as we walked out to my car.

"Of course, sweetheart, I love you too." He smiled and ended the call. "Right then, lets hit the road."

Joining the motorway at almost three in the afternoon was never going to be easy. The plan was to drive to Windsor and take a train into the city. I have to be honest, it had been so long since I was last in London, I was a little excited, plus getting away from everything felt like a weight had lifted from my shoulders no matter how brief it would be. Knowing that Natasha was out of the UK made the trip to London slightly more appealing and I suppose a night away from home was as good as a rest. I knew I'd miss Kelsey and Harry, but I was looking forward to a night without being woken by a crying toddler and after the week I had had, the concept of a good night's sleep seemed a piece of heaven at that point.

We got to the train station in Windsor just after seven. The Press had been out of service all afternoon and they were waiting for us, so we had to make it to the office. I had only spoken with them on the phone, some had visited the Blandford office, but not all of them. I wondered if Jason was the jumped up twat I had him pegged as and if Stephanie was the small and tiny retro chick I thought she was.

Once we got to Waterloo we changed to a tube train and headed across to the Embankment, our head office was about a five or ten minute walk from Big Ben overlooking the Thames.

The city buzzed with life and lit up with bright neon lights everywhere we looked. Black taxi cabs raced the streets and red double decker buses crammed the roads emitting their diesel fumes as we hastily walked towards the office.

I pulled the glass door to The Press' head office, open. We were greeted by an attractive girl with brown hair and bright red lipstick sitting behind a lard counter with 'The Press' in black written on the front. The foyer was huge with light coloured, marble floors and warm lights everywhere I looked. Two huge yucca plants stood either side of the main door and the place smelled clean and of disinfectant.

"Mr Walker, so good to see you again," she said.

"Emily, nice to see you too," Mark smiled. "This is Jeremy Buxton."

"Oh," she grinned, "I have heard a lot about you."

"Great," I smiled wryly.

"All good things, I hope." Mark added.

"Let's put it this way, if we do go ahead with the calendar for charity we were considering, I hope you will be our Mr July." She winked one of her warm, brown eyes.

"Jeremy would love to volunteer for that," Mark chuckled. "Wouldn't you?"

"Yes, of course." I swallowed and tried to smile.

"Is Brian in his office?" Mark asked.

"Yes, he is waiting for you." She answered.

"This way, Jeremy," Mark stated and walked through a large wooden door.

The office was huge compared to ours. I could see the bigger picture now in respects to the company and it shocked me to see the full size of it. Desks filled the floor from one end to the other and ad behind every desk, sat a person, working. "Pick your jaw up, Jeremy," Mark chuckled.

"I had no idea." I said gazing around. "It's massive."

"We have been here for thirty years, the Blandford office was opened by Bob Michaelson as he wanted an office in Dorset for when he was staying down there with his wife's family. That's only been open there for six years." He explained as he led me through the office. A few eyes looked up at us. Some smiled, others frowned, but they weren't malice frowns, just confusion I think.

We finally arrived at the door to another office, Mark knocked once and pushed it open.

"Mark," a deep, male voice announced, "come in, come in." I followed Mark inside. "And Jeremy, I presume."

"Yes," I smiled slightly.

"This is Brian Flanagan," Mark explained.

I knew who he was, but I had never met him face to face. "Nice to finally meet you," I said shaking his hand keenly. The man was a genius, why he wasted his talent on copy editing was beyond me.

"And you, son, and you." His silver grey hair rest on the collar of his white shirt and his small, metal framed glasses edged his deep blue eyes. He looked tired though, I could see the stress he was feeling, "We managed to get it working about half an hour ago, but if you wouldn't mind running a system check, I would appreciate it. I'd hate for it to crash again."

"We can do that," Mark nodded.

"Great, I bet you two could use a hot drink."

"A coffee would be nice," Mark smiled.

"Coffee for you too, Jeremy?" he asked.

"Yes, thank you," I smiled slightly.

He pulled his door open, "Follow me, lads." He smiled. We followed him down the corridor to a large canteen.

We made coffees using the hot water tanks like we had at our office and sat at a table while Brian explained all that had happened and how they managed to fix it. He had tried to call Mark, but it seemed we were on the tube or something, because the call never came through.

After our coffees I assisted Mark while he ran numerous system checks, checking the printers and ensuring that everything was running how it should. We met a few more staff, chatting with them about the Dorset branch and the others in the team. Stephanie was nothing like I imagined, she was very tall and slim with long blonde hair and an infectious laugh, but Jason, yes Jason was the jumped up, arrogant twat I always thought he was, his aftershave stank and he bit his fingernails way too short. I don't know why I felt threatened by him, I suppose that's why I took so much notice of everything.

Mark booked us into the hotel around the corner from the office. We had a room each and after a hot shower, wrapped in a towel, I lay on the bed and called Kelsey.

"I thought you said you would call me when you got there," she snapped.

"Sorry, sweetheart, I just wanted to make sure we got the job done so I can come home." I explained. "Is Harrison okay?"

"He is cutting teeth, but Stuart and I coped." She replied flatly.

"I will make this up to you," I promised.

"Oh, I know you will," she retorted. "I love you," she said after a few moments of silence. "And I miss you."

"I miss you too."

"You do realize this is the first night we have spent apart since Harrison was at Southampton General."

"I know," I frowned, remembering how scared we both were and how upset she was when I had to leave her there to go back to work. "We are leaving as soon as we have had breakfast, okay? I'll be home by twelve."

"I will be at work until two." She moaned.

"Well then, you had better make sure your mum can keep Harrison for a couple of hours extra."

"Why?" she asked.

"Because I am going to make love to you all afternoon," I grinned.

"Oh, is that right?" she asked timidly.

"Yes it is," I continued, "I am going to take off your knickers with my teeth," just the thought of it aroused me.

"And then what are you going to do?" she asked coyly.

"I am going to kiss and lick every inch of your body until you scream my name."

"I'll um, I'll ask Mum to watch him for a couple of extra hours then." She promised.

"Are you in bed?" I asked as I throbbed between my legs.

"Sort of, it's cold on your side and ever so lonely."

"Just the thought of you in nothing but a nightie is turning me on," I admitted.

"Jeremy, is this your attempt of phone sex?"

"I don't know, is it working?" I asked.

"Maybe," I could tell she was smiling. "I'm not even wearing a nightie," she added.

"Are you naked?" I asked, getting more excited by the second.

"I have just got out of the bath, so I am sat here with a towel wrapped around my body."

"Oh my God, I just got out of the shower, so I am also in nothing but a towel," I smiled. "You have no idea of what you are doing to me." I groaned gazing at my crotch as it began to lift the towel.

"Well," she giggled, "I could, you know, I could touch myself."

"Now you are talking," I grinned smoothing my hand over my erection. I could hear her groaning down the phone.

"Ooooh, that feels so good," she moaned and just as it was getting intense, when my head throbbed with my crutch and heat raced through my loins, I heard Harry screaming in the background.

"Bugger," she grumbled. "Sorry love, I suppose I'll have to finish massaging my feet again in the morning."

"Ha, ha, ha," I chuckled, "I love you, Mrs Buxton," I declared.

"I love you too," she said. "Goodnight, babe, see you tomorrow."

"Goodnight, my sexy minx." I grinned as my pulse slowed and the throbbing appeased. How the hell was I going to sleep now?

Eleven

Kelsey

I felt mean for not playing along with Jeremy, I lay there in the darkness missing him like crazy, not being able to sleep and hornier than I had been in months. The thought that I was turning him on warmed me from the inside out.

So I lay there, thinking about him, alone in a hotel room in London, cold, lonely and tired. I tried so hard to sleep and as soon as I began to drift away, Harry started crying again.

By the time my alarm went off the following morning, I had had about three hours sleep. I was absolutely shattered.

I didn't like to leave him with my mum when he was so irritable and in pain, but she assured me he would be fine and told me to go to work. Not only was it meant to be my day off, I was only going in because we were so short staffed and Sue had asked. I asked my mum if she minded looking after Harrison until at least four, and she was fine, surprisingly. The prospect of afternoon sex with my husband placed excitement in my tummy and kept me going all morning.

I had a couple of complexed complaints to deal with that morning and the work seemed unending and arduous. Sue could see how tired I was and just after twelve, she told me to go home and go to bed, she appreciated the fact that I had gone in, but could clearly see how knackered I was.

I literally shook in trepidation for the afternoon that lay ahead of me. There is one thing I could say about my husband, he certainly treated me well between the sheets. I had only ever slept with one other and to be honest we didn't sleep, we had sex against the wall of my flat so it was hardly a romantic love making session. I felt so bad after because I had used him. At the time I wanted to feel anything but the pain and hurt I felt, sex didn't change what had happened, my heart was in pieces, but it certainly took my mind of it for a little while.

With Jeremy, every time felt as good as the first time. He literally shook my soul and made my body quake. The thought of his soft and succulent lips kissing my body all over made me smile and my eyes twinkle, I could feel it. As I drove home the excitement grew and nothing made me feel happier than seeing his car on the drive.

I took a deep breath before opening the front door, I could hear the shower running upstairs, so I locked the door, kicked off my high heels and tiptoed up the stairs. I could see him showering through the glass door, washing his hair and the soapy water running all over his body. Covering his firm backside and down his hairy legs in white foamy suds. I quickly stripped off my clothes, and pulled open the shower door. He turned and smiled,

"Room for one more?" I asked.

"Of course," he said and moved back so I could join him. As I turned around he folded his arms around me and kissed me deeply. I could feel his arousal press against my hip as he kissed my neck and shoulders. "I couldn't sleep last night." He said between kisses.

"Me neither," I replied as he pressed his lips against my neck. "Your phone call left me all horny." I complained.

"Me too," he smiled.

"You could have, you know, taken care of yourself."

"I could have, but I haven't since I met you so, well, maybe once or twice. What about you though? You could have too."

"Maybe I did," I smiled.

"Hearing that drives me crazy." He admitted. I hadn't, but I liked that the thought of it turned him on. I took his hand and rubbed it down my body, pushing his fingers into me. "You really are horny, aren't you?"

"What are you going to do about it?" I asked breathlessly.

"Baby, you just relax and let me do all of the work." He smiled before dropping his mouth on to mine, sweeping his tongue around, tasting me as his fingers moved inside of me. Oh yes, this was not going to take long at all.

He turned me around so that I was facing away from him, pressing me against the cold, wet tiles. He pushed inside of me from behind, taking my breasts in his hands. While kissing and nipping at my shoulder, the waves of pure pleasure began to ripple through my body. My nerves burst into life, as the hot water pelted against our bodies, his legs pinning mine apart and each deep and sensual thrust made me want to bite him, it was that intense. Within moments a spine tingling orgasm rushed through my body like a tidal wave sparking each nerve alight.

He didn't stop though, his orgasm still hadn't peaked, but when it did, he groaned, pushing deep into me, squeezed my hips and sinking his teeth into my shoulder.

"Ouch!" I chuckled.

"Oh, God," he sighed loudly, "sorry, I couldn't help it." He gently kissed where he had bitten me, soothing the slightly sore skin. As we separated I turned to face him. His eyes were smouldering with desire. "Shall we take this to the bedroom?" he asked.

"Let me shower first," I smiled.

"Allow me," he said lifting my shampoo and squeezing some into his hand. As he massaged my scalp, goose bumps covered my already sensitive body. After rinsing my hair, he then conditioned it. As his fingers caressed and massaged my scalp, my arousal began to grow again. I lifted his shower gel and squeezed some into my hand, I smoothed the soap over his body, feeling every muscle, every contour; stroking his erect nipples under my palms as I smoothed my hands over his chest, down his torso towards his erection, amazed he was ready again so quickly. I took a firm, but gentle hold of him and watched as he bit his bottom lip, "Sweetheart," he groaned, "what are you trying to do to me?" he asked.

"I just want you at my mercy," I smiled and let him go. I allowed the shower water to wash the soap away and before he could move, I kneeled on the floor of the shower and for the first time since our first Christmas together, I took him into my mouth. Jeremy said that he would cum too fast when I tried this before, I wanted to tease him rather than bring him to orgasm, I didn't want to ruin it for him, so as I moved my head slowly, I squeezed his backside, pushing my nails into his flesh just enough to take his mind off the blow job.

"Oh, my God, love," he groaned, pushing his hands into my hair. I had a lot of experience at this and when I knew he was about to burst, I pulled my mouth from him. I looked up as he gazed down at me, "Wow," he gleamed. "That was pretty close."

"I know," I smiled and stood, I allowed my mouth to fill with shower water and allowing it to fall from my lips, I moved towards him and kissed him tenderly. "Let's go to bed."

Naked and dripping with water, we hurried to the bedroom and closed the door. I lifted the quilt and climbed under it. He was already beside me by the time I lay my head on the pillow.
He began kissing my neck, over my shoulders and down to my breasts, taking his time to caress each nipple with his tongue. He continued south on my body, gently kissing my stomach and my pelvis, stopping just above my pubic hair. He looked up and smiled,
"Now it's my turn," he said.

Before I could say a word, his tongue swept over me, I groaned as he moved around me, reaching deep within my core and setting my soul on fire, a fire of burning desire where I almost ached with the sheer intensity. I grabbed his hair and lifted my pelvis off the bed, just as I balanced on that delicate, mind shattering brink, he pulled his tongue from within me and dragged it slowly up my body.

While throbbing with my heartbeat, he climbed over me and nestled between my legs, he grinned smugly as I gazed up at him,
"Make love to me," I pleaded.
"How much do you want me?" he asked coyly.
"More than anything," I answered.
He pushed closer, but not quite entering me, "Are you sure?"
"Oh my God, seriously, I want you and I need you, now!"
"Need me like?"
"Like a desert needs rain, like an alcoholic needs vodka," I smiled.
"You say the most amazing thigs," he grinned again.
"If you don't get on with it, you can have another night of not sleeping because you are too horny." I replied smugly.
"In that case," he slid up my body pushing inside of me and kissed me deeply.

We made love as the early autumn sun beamed through the window in an orange glow. He took his time and I drank every second of him in. To say we were completely in love that afternoon would be an understatement. He was mine and I was his, we owned each other and as our exhausted bodies lay draped in each other with a cotton sheet covering our damp bodies, we slowly began to calm and I felt like this was our piece of heaven.

The night of lying alone thinking about what I was going to do with him only added to the excitement. The thought of what he had planned for us drove me wild all day, even though I was tired, nothing would have stopped me that afternoon.

"I have to ask," he said as his fingers stroked my arm lying across his body. "Did you, you know, take care of yourself last night?" I looked up to his eyes, I could see the thought was driving him wild. "Did you?"

"Mmm," I grinned, "now that would be telling."

"You can be such a tease," he complained playfully.

"And you love it."

"I love you," he smiled slightly, but I caught a slight glimpse of sadness in his eyes. "I will love you until my last breath, until the moon and stars fall from the sky. I will love you infinitely; never forget that, my love."

"I won't, I love you too." He swallowed hard before kissing me softly. Something was on his mind, but I would not allow it to ruin our afternoon.

Comfortable and warm, I tried very hard not to fall asleep, but with the lack of sleep the night before, I guess it was a battle I had no hope of winning. He held me tightly as we slept, his lips pressed against my shoulder and our hands linked with woven fingers. He smelled sensational and I actually thanked God that afternoon for bringing him into my life.

Luckily, Jeremy's phone rang out about an hour or so later, waking us both sharply. Though I felt groggy, I got up and after another quick shower; I dressed in jeans and a jumper before going down the stairs. To where Jeremy had made us a cup of tea and put some bread in the toaster to make some toast. He left the kitchen and hurried up the stairs.

When Jeremy finally joined me again he was now fully dressed, but he looked a little stressed, again, not wanting to upset our good moods, I said nothing as I placed a plate of toast in front of him and smiled. As I went to walk away he took my hand in his and pressed his lips against my wrist.

"Jeremy," I frowned, as he seemed to linger there, "is everything okay?"

"No, actually, it isn't." he answered. His bluntness and honesty surprised me.

"Should I be worried?" I asked.

"I don't know," he muttered and lowered his eyes. Fear began to writhe inside, bubbling like a cauldron. "Look, I have to tell you something and I know you are going to go ballistic, but I..." The front door opened followed by Stuart and Elliot coming in, laughing over something. I stared at my husband, puzzled as to what he was about to tell me and why he seemed so upset by it.

"Jezza," Stuart announced boldly, "can you do us a favour, mate?"

"Yeah," Jeremy answered and looked at me.

"Give us a lift into town, we're going to watch a film and then we are going to get absolutely rat-arsed, is that all right?"

"Of course," Jeremy nodded.

"Cheers, mate." Stuart grinned lifting a piece of Jeremy's toast. He took a bite and frowned, "What the hell is on this?"

"Lactose free butter," I replied.

"Bloody hell, that is rank." He groaned, spat it out into his hand and put it into the bin. "I really feel for you," he said turning back to us.

"Some of us don't have a choice," Jeremy sighed.

"Can't you eat normal butter?" Elliot asked.

"No, I can't have anything with milk in it," Jeremy explained.

"Blimey, that must be horrible." He frowned.

"Been like it since birth," Jeremy shrugged and stood. "I'll put my shoes on and I will be right with you boys." He said and left the kitchen.

"I need to change my shirt," Stuart added and left the kitchen.

I sighed loudly and sipped my tea, "You can sit down," I told Elliot.

"Thanks," he smiled and sat in Jeremy's chair.

"So, you and Stuart are getting on well."

"Yeah," he nodded, "can I tell you something?" he asked.

"Yes," I nodded.

"I think I am in love with him, but all he does is talk about that bloody Luke." He grumbled.

"You are in love with him?" I smiled.

He nodded his head, "Don't tell him, I don't want to put any pressure on him."

"You should tell him, Elliot, he's a great guy and maybe if you did, he would stop obsessing over his ex." I suggested.

"I don't know how to, I uh, I have never had a boyfriend before, so…"

"He's your first?" I gasped.

"Yes, something else you can't tell him. He thinks I am experienced, truth is, I only came out about six months ago and have been in hiding since."

"Elliot, you should trust Stuart, he will look after you, I promise."

"Postman," Stuart said entering the kitchen. Elliot sat up in his seat. "All for you, love," he said handing me the pile.

"Thank you," I sighed and began sifting through the envelopes.

"Oh, I am looking at a flat on Monday, can I put you and Jezza down for a reference?"

"You know you can," I nodded not looking up from the mail. I stopped sifting when I found an NHS letter, it was for Harrison. I held the envelope in my hand just staring at it, wondering if this was the letter to tell us they wanted to operate on Harrison.

"I'm ready," Jeremy said from the door. "Are you coming with us, love? We can pick Harry up on the way home." I nodded and stood still clutching the letter. I picked my bag up from the floor in the hall and slid the letter inside. I decided it would be better to open it at my mother's.

We dropped Stuart and Elliot off in town by the cinema. Jeremy asked if I was okay and I nodded. I was scared if I am honest. The thought that they wanted to operate on Harrison petrified me. Although the hospital had said they would wait until he was three, I wondered if his last infection was more serious than we first thought.

When we arrived at my mother's I showed Jeremy the letter,

"Oh," he frowned, he felt the same as I did. "But you haven't opened it."

"I can't," I admitted, "what if… what if…?"

He took it from my hand and tore it open. I watched as his incredible blue eyes scanned the page,

"It's just a routine check-up," he said folding the letter and sliding it back into the envelope.

"Bloody hell," I sighed and opened the car door. "I am so stupid."

"No you're not, you are a mother who cares about her child," he smiled and took my hand as I joined him, "come on, gorgeous, let's get our little man and go for a pizza."

I felt so relieved, but a small part of me secretly hoped that it was his operation so that they could make him better again.

Twelve

Jeremy

I couldn't wait to get home, rip my wife's clothes off and make sweet, sweet love to her. That phone call kept me awake for most of the night and left me irritated when I woke sharply the following morning after only a few hours of sleep. I ate a small bowl of fruit salad.

"Is that all you are having?" Mark asked.

"It's all I can have really, I don't like bacon and the eggs probably have milk in them, cereal is out and so is the yoghurt."

"Oh, yeah, I forgot." He frowned and laid his knife and fork down.

"Mark, its fine, I am used to it. Eat your breakfast."

"I feel guilty though." He grumbled.

"I'm not that hungry anyway." I shrugged.

"Have some toast, at least."

"I honestly just want this," I said lifting a spoonful of grapes and apple to my mouth.

"No wonder you are so bloody skinny." He scoffed. "What do you do about calcium, you must be deficient in it?"

"I take a supplement, I just can't risk anymore attacks, that last one almost landed me in the operating theatre." I explained.

"Of course, is there anything I could get you, at work, like maybe lactose free milk or…?"

I shook my head, "That stuff is bloody awful, I'd rather stick to black tea and coffee." I insisted.

"Well, let me know if you do."

"I will, thanks," I nodded.

I almost told him about Natasha, but saw no point at that moment in time, she would not destroy everything I had and by hurrying home to my wife was yet another nail in that bitch's coffin.

I wanted to be fresh and clean for her, so I shaved and took a shower so that I could be ready for her when she got home. I had no idea that she had arrived early or the fact she had come into the bathroom until the shower door opened and she climbed in with me.

We had the hottest sex we had ever had in that shower, it was so intense it gave me a head ache. She moaned and cried out as I made her climax; she scraped her nails over my back and nipped at my neck and body when we took it into the bedroom, then exhausted and spent we drifted off to sleep briefly.

My phone rang not more than an hour later, I sat up and answered it.

"Hello?" I groaned.

"Hello, stranger," Natasha said. I pushed the sheet off my body and stood. Kelsey sat up and left the room wrapping her robe around her body. "Not very talkative, are you?"

"Why are you calling me?" I demanded trying to pull my boxers up my legs. Jamming the phone against my ear with my shoulder, I dressed quickly and hurried down the stairs.

"I miss you," she replied. "I bought something special in New York for us."

"What? There is no and never will be an 'us', so get that out of your thick skull," I snapped angrily as I walked into the kitchen.

"Where's the little wifey, at work?"

I smirked, "Actually, we have just spent the day making love, so she is showing off her body ready for round six, or is it seven, fuck, who is counting?"

I heard her sigh, "You will be sorry for that," she warned eventually.

"Why?" I asked.

"Do not have sex with her again." She ordered.

"Sod off!" I barked. "She is my wife and I love her and if I wanted to shag her brains out day in and day out, it is bugger all to do with you. So, get yourself your own man and get the fuck out of my life. I don't want you; I don't even like you so how can you expect me to have sex with you? Just the thought of it makes me feel sick." She ended the call and I blew out a long relieved breath, before filling the kettle and putting it on, I suppose I hoped she's finally got the message, but not seconds later she sent a text.

'I forgive you and I won't text her the pictures if you meet me.'

Angrily I texted back, *'Shove the pictures up your stuck up arse and leave me the hell alone, you got that?'*

'If that's how you want to play.' She responded. I could hear Kelsey coming down the stairs so I made her a cup of tea and began toasting some bread. When she got to the kitchen my phone buzzed in my pocket, I hurried up to our room out of the way before pulling it out. I read her text,

'Dear Kelsey, I don't know how to tell you this, but Jeremy and I have been having an affair. It started while we were working on the contracts and he has been sleeping with me ever since. I have told him to talk to you, but he refuses, he doesn't want to hurt you, but I think it will hurt you more if you are left in the dark. He is not who you think he is. Please call me if you have to, I am happy to tell you everything - I will text this to her in three days, so you had better make up your mind. You have had enough time, it's me or her.'

Shit! My legs collapsed under me and I sat on the corner of our unmade bed. I had to tell Kelsey everything, time had run out and the inevitable approached too fast.

I could barely swallow when I came back to the kitchen, I sat silently at the table and she placed a plate of toast in front of me. I wanted to eat, but I knew I would not be able to swallow one bite. I took hold of her hand and held her wrist against my lips, drinking in her scent and allowing her soft skin to comfort me while fighting my tears, how could I break her heart?

"Jeremy," she frowned, "is everything okay?"

"No, actually, it isn't." I replied. I closed my eyes, I had to do this, I had to tell her. Maybe she would understand, maybe she would believe me, I had never given her reason not to, had I?

"Should I be worried?" she pressed, I looked up to her meeting her eyes, the fear was already building inside of her, I could see it.

"I don't know," I grumbled and lowered my eyes. "Look, I have to tell you something and I know you are going to go ballistic, but I…" The front door opened followed by Stuart and Elliot coming in, laughing over something. I let go of her wrist and flicked my eyes up to meet hers again, I had started something now and I was too bloody gutless to end it.

I agreed to drop Stuart and Elliot off in town, hurried up to our room and texted Natasha back.

'Don't do anything stupid, I'll meet you.'

'When?' came right back.

'Soon.' I replied.

'Okay,' she then sent back, *'I will make you smile, promise :).'*

We dropped Stuart and Elliot off in town and I expected Kelsey to ask me a thousand questions, but none came, something was bothering her and it scared me to think that it might have been me. That was right up until she showed me the letter from the hospital. I took it from her and tore it open. It was a check-up appointment, but I knew what was going through her mind, it flashed through mine also. The operation that Harry had to have had a fifty-fifty chance of survival and a fifty-fifty chance of being successful, it may not cure him and it could kill him. I didn't like the odds, but without it he would definitely die. But a check-up was manageable, at that moment, I could cope with that.

Harry was in great spirits, he had apparently slept all afternoon which could only mean one thing, a late night for us. We got home after five, the evening was already drawing in and the air felt cool against my skin as I carried Harry inside. Kelsey bought in his bag,

"Cars, Daddy," Harry yelled as soon as I put him down on the floor. He ran into the living room and I could hear him rooting through his toy box looking for his cars. It was something we did together whenever we could and I suppose as I had been away for a night, it was his way to show me he had missed.

Lying on the rug in front of the TV, we played for hours. Kelsey sorted the laundry out and after deciding against pizza, she began preparing dinner as we pushed cars around his garage on the rug. He made me laugh so hard when he made the brum-brum noises by basically blowing raspberries and dribbling all over the front of him.

"Dinner's ready," Kelsey said from the door. I looked up, "Are you okay?"

"Yeah, have you heard him play cars?" I asked with a lump of emotion building in my throat.

"He is pretty funny when he plays, have you seen his white car?" she asked with a warm smile.

I lifted the white car, "This one?"

"Daddy's car," Harry announced and took it from my hand.

"Aww," Kelsey gushed.

"He is a clever little chap, isn't he?"

"He is so much like you," she smiled, "it's like I have two of you to love." I stood from the floor and lifted Harry.

"And you get two of us to love you back." I said as I walked towards her, planting a small kiss on her lips, I felt her smile under my lips.

After dinner I bathed Harry and put him into his pyjamas, even though he was nowhere near ready for bed, at least he was dressed for it. He continued to play with his toys while I sat glaring at the TV. I couldn't stop thinking about having to meet up with Natasha. I didn't want to, but I didn't want her to send that text to Kelsey, so it seemed I had no choice.

We finally got Harry to sleep just after ten, which gave Kelsey and I an hour before we had to go to bed ourselves. I sat beside her on the couch and put my arm around her, pulling her into my body.

"I got so scared when I saw that letter, Jeremy." She admitted weaving her fingers with mine.

"I know sweetheart, if I am honest, I was a bit scared too." I admitted. "But, it would be nice to get it over and done with, you know? I feel like it's a ticking time bomb waiting to go off. Winter is coming and neither of us can afford to catch a cold or get the flu, it would put him back in the hospital again if he caught it."

"I know what you mean," she nodded and sat silently for a few moments. "This afternoon was amazing, by the way, I never got to say thank you."

I smiled, "You don't have to thank me, it was the best sex we've had in months," I added.

"Well, at least I know I can um…you know… go down on you and it not um…well, you know, like last time." Heat flushed my face. "Sorry."

"Don't be sorry, it was amazing," I grinned.

"I told you I have had a lot of practice." She added coyly.

"You certainly have skills my dear wife, that's the longest I have gone without… well anyway, no woman has ever been able to do that for me," I chuckled.

"I don't like to brag, but Kyle never complained." She giggled.

"I bet he didn't," I grumbled playfully.

"Aww, are you getting jealous?" she teased.

"I hate to think of him touching you."

"That's how I feel about you, I mean, you know there was only Kyle before, I have no idea how many women you slept with before me." Ouch! I sat up and fidgeted in my seat. "Sorry, its none of my business."

"Fourteen, to the best of my knowledge, there could be a few more, though I would have been totally trashed so wouldn't remember."

"Fourteen women?" she sat up and turned to face me. I nodded my head shamefully. "Wow, fourteen, I had no idea you were in the teens."

"Sorry," I sighed.

"Can you remember their names?" she asked.

"Why do you want to know their names?" I frowned.

"I just do," she shrugged taking my hand in hers, "please tell me."

I thought for a few moments, "If you are sure?" I checked, she nodded her head, "Well, you know about Amanda, after her there was a girl called Crystal, Giles' cousin, remember the arsehole who groped you?" She nodded again. "Um, let me see, Shelly, Alexandra, Chantel, Emma, she was at college," I smiled, she was actually a sweet girl and I ruined her. "Claire, Zoe, Rhianna, Inaya, Cassandra, Phoebe, Tara and then you, the love of my life." The colour drained from her face slightly, "I might have had a few notches in my belt, love, but I have never cheated on any of them. I never went behind anyone's back or anything like that. I would never do that."

"Why do you keep saying never?" she asked.

"I just need you to understand that I am not that kind of bloke."

"Sweetie, if I thought that, I would never have married you." She leaned towards me and kissed my lips.

As she pulled back she gazed into my eyes, so I added, "And none of them could ever make me feel the way I do when I make love to you. With them it was just sex, but with you, it's like our souls connect and that makes us extremely special."

"Don't forget about the incredible head," she winked.

"No chance of that," I smiled.

After a cup of tea we headed to bed, both of us had work the following day and although I knew I would have to meet with Natasha, I fell asleep with no problems at all.

I kissed Kelsey goodbye and headed to work. The golden autumn sun hun low in a bright blue sky and as we were only days away from Halloween, I noticed the cooler air as soon as I stepped outside.

Arriving at the office early, I logged on to my computer to discover an email from Natasha. I was about to delete it when Sebastian came bouncing in and placed an envelope on the desk in front of me, I looked up at him, he smiled crookedly,

"As the best, best man a groom could ever need, you are cordially invited to our official engagement party on Halloween," he announced proudly.

"Oh, right." I nodded.

"Are you alright, cuz?"

"Look at this," I said handing him my phone. He scrolled through the messages and frowned.

"You have got to do something about this, Jez, do not let it get any worse."

"You don't think I know that," I sighed. "What can I do, if I meet her she wins, if I don't she wins, I am shafted anyway you look at it."

"Maybe you should just shag her then, get it over with, pin her up against a wall and give her what she wants."

"You may not believe this, but I am not attracted to her in the slightest, just the thought of that turns my stomach."

"She is bloody gorgeous, mate, are you sure?" he asked.

"I am positive, I have all I need with my wife," I replied adamantly.

"In that case, you need shot of her and we need a plan." He stood from my desk, "Let me think about it, don't meet with her yet, we need to work something out, alright?" I nodded glumly. "Look, she's screwed up by sending you these messages, this is documented proof." He added. "I'm making a cuppa, want one?"

I nodded and handed him my mug, "Cheers," I muttered.

"Don't worry about it, I will be there with you, Kelsey will listen to me."

"Yeah, cos, she's always listened to you before," I scoffed.

It was nice to know that I wasn't in this alone, that, as always, Seb would be by my side. Even if I lost my wife, I would still have Seb. Just the thought of it made me feel sick, but it was a possibility and had to except that. If she had a situation like mine, where a good looking guy was blackmailing her into having an affair, I was bloody positive I wouldn't believe her.

Thirteen

Kelsey

I gazed at the computer screen and smiled, the day before had been absolutely incredible and I already had plans in my head for that evening. The more my husband gave to me, the more I wanted. I had a thirst and I needed it quenching. Sue had moved me back to my team after checking with management if that was okay. I was both happy and relieved to be back at my old desk.

"Right, Kelsey?" Shawna asked. I snapped back to reality, I was sat at my desk in an 'idle' code on the phone so that no calls could come through and interrupt my daydreaming about that sensual afternoon with my incredible husband.

"Sorry, what?" I frowned.

"Sebastian and Jude will be okay with money?" she checked.

"Money for what?"

"Their engagement, my invite came through yesterday, they are having a massive Halloween ball at Buxton Manor on Saturday night," she grinned. "I did tell you."

"Oh, I know," I nodded, I couldn't think why we hadn't been invited. "I suppose money will be fine, but I am sure they don't really want anything." I stood from my desk, "I am going for a coffee, would anyone else like one?"

"I'd love a latte," Nicki said holding out her money.

I took her money, "Okay," I said and left them in the office.

I waited for our drinks and got myself a bag of Malteasers while I waited. "Are you okay?" Nicki asked from behind.

"No, I am bloody annoyed." I replied. "I am meant to be Jude's best friend, I even met her in town and we still haven't got an invite."

"She probably thinks that you don't need an invite." She shrugged.

"Well, we won't be there if we don't get one," I retorted and handed her a cup of smoking latte.

"Thanks." She smiled and sipped her drink while I waited for mine.

"What's this, a mother's meeting?" Lou announced from the door, Nicki and I turned to face her, "Sorry, what's up, babes?"

"Her invite hasn't arrived yet," Nicki explained thinly.

"I haven't got mine either," she smiled and hugged me. Smelling incredible, in fact I recognised the scent.

"Oh my God, you got that free sample of Fabreeze too?" I asked pulling back from her.

"What?" she frowned and looked at Nicki.

"Jeremy said we got this new scent through the door, it was so nice he filled the house with it, it smells amazing." I explained.

"If you are referring to my perfume, it is that new one for Deere, it costs something like sixty quid a bottle, not some free sample from Fabreeze and if it is that, I want a refund."

"Yeah, Kelsey," Nicki added. "It's really expensive perfume."

"So, either your nose is mistaken or Jeremy has had a woman in your house and she wears expensive perfume." Lou frowned.

"Have his sisters been to visit or something?" Nicki asked.

"No," I shook my head, he would not have lied to me. "It's probably me," I shrugged, lifted my drink from the machine and headed back to my desk.

It made perfect sense when I really thought about it, all of the extra sex, the effort he put in to pleasing me, telling me a hundred times or more how much he loved me, was it out of guilt? Had he been seeing another woman behind my back? More to the point, had he been seeing a certain socialite that happened to be a millionaire and the daughter of the owner of three of the biggest magazines in the industry?

I felt so sick at the thought that all the late night dinners he had been to with her may not have been just for business. The lies he was telling if that was the case. The more I thought the more it made sense. Who was I? I was just his wife, the mother of his child, I hadn't had my hair or nails done in months and up until recently the only action we saw between the sheets was when Harrison had been sick and slept in with us.

But this was Jeremy, he may have been gorgeous, but I found it hard to believe that he would lie to me, especially as it would mean that last few weeks were all lies. I had jumped to conclusions and by home time I decided that just because she may have been to our house and he may have had a couple of dinners with her, it did not mean he was having an affair. Jeremy would not do that to me. Would he?

My dismissive mood lasted right up until I collected Harrison from my mother's and went grocery shopping. We needed a lot of food as the freezer was now empty and Jeremy had taken the last of the bread for sandwiches at work. As I drifted down the aisles, not really paying much attention to anything, I couldn't stop wondering what if I was wrong, what if he was cheating on me, what if?

"Kelsey?" A voice broke into my thoughts, "Is that you?" I looked up, Felix grinned. I hadn't seen him in months and I don't know why, but I dived into his arms and hugged him. "Are you alright?"

"Yes, sorry," I smiled slightly as we parted. Embarrassed by my actions I looked at Harrison trying to bite at the grapes through the packaging, "How are you?"

"I am good," he nodded. "He's grown loads since I last saw him." he said motioning his head the Harrison.

"You should hear him talk," I nodded.

"He'll be chasing girls before you know it. Just like his old man." He chuckled. I just stared, if only he knew what I was thinking. "You looked like you were somewhere else," he added.

"I think I am tired," I lied.

"So, Jez texted me, you'll be at the party Saturday then."

"Oh, I didn't know we had been invited."

"He's Seb's best man, of course you'll be there." He chuckled. "Are you sure you are alright?"

I thought for a few moments, "You have known him for years, haven't you?" he nodded. "In those years, did you ever know him to… to uh, to cheat on a girlfriend?"

"No, he has never cheated on any of them, I mean, there were quite a few girls, but he only went out with one at a time, contrary to popular belief, Jez is not a cheat." He affirmed.

"Okay," I nodded, "thank you."

"What's going on?"

"Nothing," I lied. "I have to go, so maybe I will see you Saturday night then."

"Okay, Kelsey," he smiled slightly. "I'll see you Saturday."

When we got home, I tried very hard not to think about everything, but it was pointless. It kept going over in my head all the times he said he was working late, the trip to London, was it really work, or was he meeting someone? It gave me a huge headache and by the time he got home, I couldn't help but be frosty towards him. I didn't want to give him my all and get nothing back. I deserved better than that.

He had already asked my mother to babysit Saturday night and I guessed that as we were going to a party, he wouldn't want to take me out Friday night as well. Mind you, I did briefly think that it was out of guilt anyway. He seemed distant again, or maybe that is what I wanted to think. I made dinner but couldn't eat, I fed and bathed Harrison and put him to bed and then I changed into my pyjamas before heading back to the living room.

Stuart was home and sat watching TV with Jeremy, the atmosphere in the living room was so suffocating, I decided to go onto my laptop and check out what my friends were up to. I sat at the kitchen table and scrolled through my feed. I wanted to confront him, ask my husband who had been in our house and if I had anything to worry about? Was he considering leaving us, breaking my heart? I mean, it certainly wouldn't be the first time. I felt positive that my heart couldn't take another beating by Jeremy Bloody Buxton.

If he was going to leave, or wanted a relationship with *her*, why was he trying so hard to make me happy? It must have been guilt. My mind writhed all evening and because it made me feel so sick, I went to bed without even telling him.

I heard him coming up the stairs, so I squeezed my eyes closed and turned on my side. I didn't want to talk to him because at that moment, I probably would have just told him to go. I wanted to give him the chance to tell me the truth, I wanted to give him the benefit of the doubt. He was my world and I adored the very ground he walked on, but I was certain that there was no chance I would just forget about it and pretend nothing was wrong. He would eventually pick up on it and then we would talk. For now though, it was easier to pretend I was asleep.

He climbed into bed and leaned towards me, I felt his soft and succulent lips press against my cheek before he turned over. Within moments he seemed to be asleep. I lay in the dark contemplating my life without him, wondering if I would be able to face even one day without him by my side.

The night is an incredibly lonely place when you are awake with painful thoughts, fears and worries. Reliving the good times in your head and dreading the unknown. I swear I could feel my heart harden and a crust form around it as I lay there listening to him breathe. It's amazing how in one moment you are so unbelievably happy, elated and feeling totally blessed, then suddenly and without warning, you're not. It felt like he was slipping through my fingers and the concept petrified me, if I wasn't Jeremy's wife, then who was I?

By morning I had pondered and contemplated long enough. I promised to let him tell me the truth, if there was in fact anything I need to know. I waited for him to get up before pushing the covers from my body, I felt so washed out and didn't like the idea of going into the office, but I had no choice, I signed my contract and they needed me, plus it was Friday, so at least I had the weekend to look forward to, well, almost.

He left after pecking my cheek, I know he sensed something was wrong, but failed to query it. I showered and dressed and when I came down the stairs Stuart was sat at the kitchen table.

"Right," he said, "what's wrong?"

"Nothing," I shrugged.

"You look like the weight of the world is on your shoulders and the atmosphere between you two is asphyxiating."

I just heaved a sigh and sat at the table, "Do you think he is cheating on me?" I asked.

"No," he frowned, but shifted his eyes around the room; Stuart was lying to me too? "Why?"

"I came home last weekend and the most amazing scent filled the house, when I asked him, he said it was a sample of air freshener and he used it all up because it was so nice. Yesterday Lou tells me it's one of the most expensive perfumes on the market which means Jeremy has lied to me and I want to know what is going on."

"Wow, you think he is cheating on you because of a smell in the house?"

"It was on my pillow, it was in our bathroom upstairs and down, what would you think?"

"I don't know, Luke cheated on me and I never knew, but we're talking about Jez here, he wouldn't do that to you, he loves you too much." He shrugged anxiously, still unable to completely meet my eyes which could have meant that I was right and Stuart knew everything.

I sighed again, "That's one of the things most of our family and friends said about my dad after he cheated on my mother with her best friend, that he wouldn't do that to us, that he loved us and look, he did it anyway." I snapped.

"Jeremy is not your dad."

"No, he isn't, but he is no saint either." I retorted.

"Well, instead of making assumptions, perhaps you should ask him yourself." He said and stood. "The one thing that really pisses me off with you two is your inability to actually talk to each other, that's not a relationship, Kelsey." He added and left the kitchen.

I dropped Harrison off at my mother's and went to work. The morning flew by, a storm had hit the north of the country and we were the overflow for claims, so the phones buzzed all morning and before I knew it, it was time to go home. But go home to what? A house that was once filled with happiness and love now seemed an empty shell.

Our home had been damaged, the warmth and comfort I once felt there had gone, disappeared over night and now all I felt was fear. Fear that my friends all knew and I would be the last to find out the truth, fear that everything we had was gone and fear that my faith and trust would be irrevocably destroyed.

I collected Harrison after work and Mum mentioned Saturday night, the elusive party of which I still hadn't been properly invited to. Jeremy hadn't said anything to me about it and I wondered if he wanted me to go. I arrived home already tied up in knots and my stomach running two to the dozen. The thought that I could lose him was already breaking my heart and he hadn't even said anything yet.

The phone was ringing when I got inside, I put Harrison down so he could run and play and lifted the receiver.

"Hello?" I said. Nothing. "Hello?" I said again, still nothing. I hung up the phone and put my keys on the table beside the stairs. As I went to walk away it rang again, "Hello?" I said more forcefully.

"Can I speak with Miss Buxton please?" a voice asked.

"Speaking," I answered.

"Good afternoon, my name is Sarah and I am calling from the Crown hotel in Blandford."

"Yes?" I frowned.

"I have Mr Buxton's phone here, it fell out of his pocket when you left this afternoon, someone had picked it up in the carpark." Pain shot through my body, I couldn't breathe, "I was wondering if you will be back?"

"Um, yes, of course." I swallowed, "I'll drive there now."

"Great, I'll leave it with the duty manager. Your husband is one clever cookie, if hadn't had put you down as his ICE contact, we would never have known."

"ICE?"

"Yes, In Case of Emergency."

"Oh, right, well, yes, but not so clever as to not lose his phone though," I muttered as tears pierced my eyes. "Thank you, I'll be there shortly."

I lifted my keys and called to Harrison, whether I wanted to face this or not, I had to, I had no choice. The thought that he was out with another woman riled me to the core, I wanted to thump him and scratch her eyes out, but I also wanted an explanation, maybe it was innocent. Maybe!

It took ages to find a parking space, but in all honesty, I was looking for his car. I suppose I was relieved not to see it. I hurried inside with Harrison in my arms, a young man with dark blond hair and large brown eyes, wearing a name badge called Shaun, smiled.

"I believe you have my uh, my husband's phone."

"You must be Mrs Buxton."

"That I am," I choked, straining to get my words out over my painful throat. He handed me the phone and smiled again.

"I expect it was because he was so upset."

"Sorry?" I frowned.

"Your husband, I didn't see him for long, but he didn't look very happy."

"Well, he'll be happy you found his phone." I tried to smile, my face just would not move. "Thank you." I muttered and left the hotel.

I heaved in deep breaths of fresh air when I got outside, Harrison started complaining so I strapped him into his seat and headed home. The traffic on the road home was horrendous, I hadn't been passed there in almost a year, but taking a detour past Badbury Rings was better than sitting in traffic for an hour, especially in the mood I was in.

As I got closer to the entrance I could see a car, a huge white car, registration Jez Bux1. Yes, my bloody husband's car, parked near the entrance and just off the road. I slowed my car down, furious that he would bring his 'bit of stuff' to our place, our most precious, personal place and he was there, with her. I slowed my car down even more, to almost stopping as I passed and I could see them, I could see her, beautiful, stunning and laughing, in *my* husband's car. She was laughing and he, well, he looked angry, in fact, he looked bloody furious, though I doubted he was. I pressed my foot down on the pedal and hurried home.

How dare they, how bloody dare they do this to me? Me, the stupid cow, the idiot believing every sodding word that came out of his mouth. Anger turned quickly to despair and before long I could hardly see the road for tears.

What the hell was I going to do?

Fourteen

Jeremy

What a difference a day makes? Wednesday I spent most of the afternoon making love to my wife and then it all changed. Thursday she barely said a word to me. Okay, maybe I was a little pissed off with Natasha and through fear of saying the wrong thing, I kept my mouth shut.

So I got the silent treatment Thursday, although I admit I had a lot on my mind, Seb's plan of trying to trap Natasha into admitting what she was doing and why she was doing it, made me feel sick to the stomach. I didn't like the idea of seeing her alone or even meeting her at all. But Seb said it would work, to be perfectly honest, it had to. I wanted this woman out of my life and Seb decided to play her at her own game, a little blackmail of my own could rid her from my life, I should have known that two wrongs never make a right.

Friday came around too fast for my liking, still, I pecked Kelsey's cheek before leaving praying that everything would be back to normal and soon. I wanted to tell her everything just in case it went wrong, but Sebastian, my ever loyal cousin, said he had my back and I trusted his intensions, even if the outcome would not be the one we both desired. I just hoped the plan worked and Natasha would disappear as quickly as she arrived in my life.

First order of the day, I had to talk to Mark, he needed to know all that had happened and even if it cost me my job, if it got rid of her, I didn't care. I drove to work in a bit of a daze, running everything over in my head and when I arrived I wondered how I made it without having an accident.

Walking into the office I think I was prepared for anything, Mark and I had a good manager, employee relationship and I had faith that he would trust me and stand behind me if I needed him to.

Apprehensively, I knocked on his door with a shaky hand and waited for him to answer.

"Morning, Jeremy," Mark said from behind, in his hand he had a cup of tea and a blue employee folder tucked under his arm.

"Do you have time for a chat?" I asked nervously.

"Sure," he nodded, "come on in." I followed him inside his office and closed the door behind me. My tie felt suddenly too tight and my top lip moistened with the warmth in the room. "Have a seat." I unbuttoned my suit jacket before sitting on the chair opposite him.

"I have something to tell you, Mark and I don't think you are going to like it," I explained.

"I am listening."

I heaved a shaky breath, "Natasha Mason is trying to ruin my life."

He looked bemused, "How?"

"Here," I pushed my phone across his desk, he lifted the phone and began reading the messages. I watched as his eyes darted across the screen and when he finished he looked up and frowned.

"Why didn't you tell me?" he asked.

"The contract."

"Yes, so what, I will not have anyone threatening my staff, I don't care who they are."

"Are you sure? Because I would resign if it made your life easier." I offered.

"Out of the question. Christ, Jeremy, you are the best copy editor I have ever had. Your eye for detail and your knowledge of grammar is astounding. Why would I ever choose a contract over that?"

"I uh, I suppose I thought that maybe the deal meant a lot to The Press."

"Yes, well, its only money and if this is how she works, then I don't want anything to do with the Masons." He scoffed and pushed my phone back to me. "What has Kelsey said?"

"I haven't spoken to her about it yet. If I had lost my job, well, I had a plan to meet with Natasha today to get her to confess, but now…"

"Oh, I would still meet her, I would get as much out of her as you can and then we can hit her father with it all. I would like to wipe the grin off his smug face for once." He smiled.

"Last time, she uh, she groped me," I explained. "She uh, grabbed me and uh… well, you know."

"Dirty little tart," he frowned.

"What if she tries something again or worse?"

"Then you can hit her with a sexual assault charge. I have a few friends at the police station, if it would help, I can get them to have a word with her."

"If she doesn't back off, I might have to take you up on that offer."

"Well, Jeremy, you are a valuable asset to this company, we would be lost without you and I will make sure Brian knows what's going on." He promised. "Now, you look like crap, go and get yourself a cuppa and a biscuit, when was the last time you ate anything?"

"Uh, Wednesday night, things have been a bit tense at home."

"Then we need this to end, today." I nodded and stood.

"Thank you, Mark. It means a lot to know you are on my side and that you believe me."

"With what that little hussy has been messaging my staff with, she's lucky I haven't spoken to her father already. Jeremy, promise me you will talk to Kelsey, she needs to hear this from you. The last thing you want is for her to find out and think you have lied to her."

"I am talking to her when I get home tonight." I promised.

I felt a bit better after speaking with him and found Seb at his desk, I told him I had Mark on my side and he suggested I text Natasha and ask to meet her lunch time at the Crown.

So with the time and place set, all I had to do now was borrow a few items from the tech department, a small camera and recorder. Sebastian helped to kit out my car and hide all of the technology. Thank God my car had Bluetooth; I was amazed at just how much could work from that alone. Twelve o'clock came and I left the office. The car was completed kitted out with technology and I felt like I was in control of the Millennium Vulcan, not my Evoque.

My heart pounded in my chest as I made my way through the carpark towards the main door. I could see her sat in window, the autumn sun glowing on her skin, if only she was as perfect as she looked. I couldn't understand why she picked me, she could have had any man she wanted and yet she chose my life to ruin.

"You're late," she snapped as I approached her table. The place was so noisy, we were virtually invisible.

"I could leave again," I stated.

"No, sit, I've ordered some lunch."

"Don't talk to me like your pet dog, I'm not hungry." I frowned as I sat opposite her. She just stared, first into my eyes, then at my platinum wedding ring, that suddenly felt as though it was strangling my finger. I envisioned Kelsey doing the same thing to my neck.

"You look tired." She remarked.

"I am, my wife is wearing me out." I lied.

"Don't," she snapped, "don't mention her, I told you to stop sleeping with her."

I smiled slightly, "I have stopped sleeping with her, that's why I am tired. We have sex all night every night at the moment." I lied.

"Just the thought of that makes me feel sick." She grumbled.

"That's how I feel when I think about what you want." I retorted angrily.

"I have you, Jeremy, I have you by the balls and you know it. That's why you are here, that's why you agreed to meet with me."

"No, this is your last chance, Natasha, that's why I am here. Leave me alone or I will go to your father."

She laughed loudly, "He doesn't give a shit about what I do, never has. I do what I want; I get what I want, when I want it." That did it, I stood from the table. "Sit down," she ordered.

"Up yours," I snapped and left. Racing for the door, hoping she would follow, because only in my car would I be able to get the evidence I needed to save what was left of my marriage.

"Jeremy, wait." She called out chasing after me. "We need to talk, I'm sorry, okay? I am sorry I spoke to you like that."

I reached my car and opened the door,

"Please, we can talk, when I tell you why, you'll understand." She begged. I turned to face her.

"Let's go for a drive," I suggested.

She hurried to the passenger door and climbed in. I got in and pulled the door shut. Adjusted my mirror to check the camera was still nestled between the seats in the back and started the engine. I sped out of the carpark to show her I was still angry and raced towards Wimborne.

"Do you have to drive so fast?" she asked.

"Kelsey never complains," I shrugged, she bloody did and I knew it. "So, come on then, why are you blackmailing me?"

"I wouldn't call it blackmail," she smiled.

"Natasha, you have threatened to tell my wife that we are having an affair even though we aren't. Even though I haven't touched you, you are blackmailing me to sleep with you. Why?"

"I can't stop thinking about you, I want you, I have since the first day I met you. There is nothing wrong with giving in to your needs." She explained.

"Your needs, not mine. I have all I need with Kelsey, she is the most incredible person I know and you are going to ruin my life for what? Sex? Is it just sex or is there something else?"

"Well, I was hoping that there would be something more between us, after. I can make you so happy, she makes you miserable, you admitted that."

"No, I said that we were having a hard time, you know my son is sick and you still want to end my marriage. I just don't get it." I explained as we drove towards Badbury Rings, Kelsey's favourite place in Dorset and a perfect spot to park the car so that I could get some more proof.

"A woman has needs too you know, I need to have a man on my arm that not only looks the part, but is the part. You are extremely handsome and have a terrific body, you are well spoken and educated, so you would make a good companion to any socialite at a ball or a function. I am sick of being on my own; I want to be for you what Kelsey is."

"Huh," I scoffed, "you could never be for me what Kelsey is, not even if she left me tomorrow. She is one of the strongest, caring, loving women in the world and do you want to know something? She doesn't even know how wonderful she is. That is why she is so amazing."

I slowed the car and pulled off the main and onto the gravel drive. At the last second, I decided to park so that we could be seen by the road. I didn't want her to think I wanted anything from her, the carpark was renowned for lovers looking for somewhere they could rendezvous virtually unseen. Even Kelsey and I had taken advantage of that.

"Do you honestly think I will just let you get away with this, with telling me all about how perfect your little wife is? She is nothing compared to me, I am worth millions and she is nothing more than a commoner. You were destined to be with someone like me, look at your life, where you have been, who you have been out with, Phoebe St. Clare and Tara, both of them are worth millions."

"Phoebe is a great girl and maybe we had something years ago, but Tara, she was fine right up until she cheated on me with my once best friend and I don't care how rich you are, it does not give you the right to cheat on someone you are supposed to care about."

"When you have money, you can do whatever you want," she shrugged.

"You can't buy love, Natasha, if you think that then I feel sorry for you."

"Don't you just want a night of pure, unadulterated fun, a no strings attached night of the steamiest sex you could ever have?" she asked.

"Actually, no, I don't. A few years back, before I met Kelsey maybe, but not anymore. When you meet the one, your soulmate, you never need or want anyone else because you have all you could ever need in that one person. She is why I get up every day and work my bloody arse off week in and out. She makes it all worth it and I am sorry, Natasha, but not even someone who is worth millions could ever equate to that."

"I could destroy that though," she grinned. "I could send that message and tell her everything."

"She already knows, we talked last night," I lied.

"Did you tell her about the hand job I gave you?"

"You mean the hand job you forced on me, the hand job I did not consent to." I corrected, "Well, you men are all alike, on touch and up it goes." She retorted.

"I still didn't consent." I stated adamantly. "I told Kelsey everything."

"What did she say?"

"She believed me, she believed that you are blackmailing me, that you forced yourself on to me. She trusts me" I shrugged.

"The stupid bimbo wouldn't even know how to process that sort of information. Let's face it, Jeremy, she's hardly Carol Vordermon." She laughed.

"Don't talk about my wife like that, she has done nothing to you, so leave her alone." I growled. My temper fuelled, this was ending and soon.

"Hit a sore nerve, have I?" she mocked.

"I am asking you to stop this, the messages and the threats, it all has to stop."

"I am only just getting started." She then grinned, "We could hop in the back, get it over with and then you can run back to your little wifey and it will all be a thing of the past."

"I wouldn't have sex with you if you were the last woman in the universe, have you got that? I hate you, just the thought of being intimate with you turns my stomach. You may look all that, but let me tell you something, sweetheart, looks aren't everything and you will look like a little old woman soon enough, I don't doubt that you'll still be single because you have no idea of what it's like to actually fall in love."

I started the engine and drove back towards Blandford. I wasn't sure if we had enough, not until we arrived back at the Crown.

She unclipped her seatbelt, "This is your last chance," she warned. "Come inside and have sex with me now or I will ruin your life."

"In the words of my dear cousin Sebastian, you have more chance of pissing petrol."

"Is that your final answer?"

"Yes, it is, I don't need to ask the audience and I certainly don't need to phone I friend. I will never have sex with you, never. I don't like you, I don't want you and if I lost everything tomorrow, I would still feel the same. I am not surprised you are single, you are pure and utter evil."

"Don't say I didn't warn you." She snarled.

"You have nothing left," I snapped. "I have spoken to Mark and I have told my wife, there is nothing you can do to me."

"We'll see about that," she retorted, "I just hope you like prison food." She slammed my car door shut and without thinking, I sped out of the carpark and headed home.

I had to talk to Kelsey before Natasha did, so I raced home and prayed that I got the chance to explain everything before Natasha contacted her. I didn't know what she meant about the prison food comment, I supposed it was just another threat. I was already one up on her, I had the backing of The Press.

When I got home, completely forgetting about the important cargo in my car, I ran inside and called out Kelsey's name.

"I'm in here," she said quietly.

I hurried to the living room, she was sat on the couch with her leg crossed over her knee and swinging it, she was pissed off.

"Are you alright?" I asked her warily.

"Yes, why wouldn't I be?" she answered frostily.

"I uh, I don't know. Where is Harry?"

"*Harrison* is at my mother's." She replied. "Why are you home so early?"

"I have something to tell you." I said cautiously, not completely sure how to take her demeanour. I sat on the arm of the chair and looked at my beautiful wife. I felt like I did the day I discovered my ex-girlfriend was pregnant after I had fallen in love with Kelsey. I felt like I was about to lose her. It caused a pain the writhe in my chest and my hands to shake, but it was time to talk to her, to tell her everything.

Then she held up my phone, "You uh, you lost this in the Crown carpark when you took your uh, whore for a ride in *our* car."

"I can explain everything." I began.

Fifteen

Kelsey

He looked so pale and tired, I almost pitied him, almost. The cheating, lying piece of shit dared to sit there and explain away the fact that he was screwing some tart behind my back. But because I couldn't get into his phone, because he has a password on the thing, I had to listen, before I told him to sod off, forever.

"Remember the dinners I had to have with Natasha Mason?" he asked. I swallowed and nodded my head. "After the last dinner there was a problem and I have been trying to work out how I tell you this. I should have from the start, but she threatened to ruin my life."

"Oh, so you fucking some socialite whore is completely her fault, is that what you are trying to tell me?" I demanded.

"Don't swear like that," he frowned.

"Excuse me, but I am furious right now, so I think I deserve to throw a few 'F' words out now and again." I retorted angrily.

"Okay, if that's how you want it. No, I am not *fucking* Natasha Mason, I never have and I never will. If you give me a few moments to explain what's going on, I'll answer any questions you want." He handed me his phone, unlocked and open on a message dating back to the Friday Stuart moved into our home. "You had better start by reading the messages she has sent me."

I scrolled through the long list of messages there were so many and as I scanned through them, my eyes felt like they were bleeding.

'Have an affair with me, or I will tell your wife.'

'Are you ready to lose everything?'

'It's just sex, we could be good together.'

I read all of what she had to say and his responses and okay, maybe he hadn't said anything in the messages to lead me to believe this was a two sided affair, I still had my doubts. He had still lied to me, lied about the perfume, lied about what was going on at work. Did he meet her in London? How many afternoons had they met and talked in his car? Had he flirted with her, shown some sort of interest in her for her to think they would have a chance at all?

"As you can see, this was her, all her, she had threatened to tell you we had slept together, even though we haven't and nothing could have been further from my mind."

"So, you never laid a finger on her, led her on or to believe that you felt the same way?"

"No," he frowned. "I have never touched her."

"Has she ever touched you?" I asked.

"Honestly?" he checked.

"Yes," I swallowed.

"That Friday, she uh, she grabbed me and…"

"Grabbed you where?" I frowned.

"Um, she grabbed my, my uh…here." He pointed to his crotch.

I felt so sick, but I had to know, "She grabbed your dick? Well, were you dressed?" I asked as tears fought with my yes and pain strained at my throat.

"Yes, it was in my car after I told her to sod off, she grabbed me and rubbed me, it uh, it made me…"

"Oh my God!" I stood. "She made you cum?" I yelled.

"Yes, but I didn't want to. I tried not to, so much so that it hurt." He admitted, I could see he was embarrassed.

"I uh, I need some air." I frowned and walked towards the door, but I wasn't finished yet. I turned back to face him, "You say nothing happened, but she did that to you, it must have turned you on." I said from the door, not looking at him, repulsed that she dare to lay a hand on him.

"No, you know what it's like for a bloke, we see a nipple through a blouse and get a hard on." He stood from the arm of the couch. "It's not something I had much control over. She grabbed me and rubbed me and all I wanted to do was puke. I fought as hard as I could until it was too late, so, ashamed and embarrassed I rushed home and took a shower. I felt dirty and degraded and that night when you came on to me, all I could see, smell and feel was her hand on me, it made me feel pathetic."

I stared at the floor, trying to take it in, she touched him, she touched my husband. "She's been here, hasn't she?" I asked. "That was the perfume in the house the Saturday after, she filled my house with her bloody scent like a cat in season spraying everywhere to make her mark." I snarled. "I felt a complete idiot when I asked if Lou had got the same Fabreeze sample we had. To be told it's an expensive perfume, I felt like a sodding bimbo."

"I didn't know what to say, I lied because at the time, I thought it would all disappear, that she would never come back. She came to the house that Saturday to tell me that she was going away, that I had a few days extra to think about her proposition. There was never anything to think about, I would never cheat on you. Never!"

I frowned, "So you say," I sighed.

"Kelsey, I have never given you a reason not to trust me," he reasoned walking towards me.

"Not until now," I admitted as I crossed my arms over my chest. He placed his hands on my shoulders and gazed into my eyes.

He lowered his head and I fought the urge to reach out and touch him. "It's all over now, I have told her to sod off for the last time. I told her that I have already spoken to Mark and that I have told you everything. I told her that she has no hold on me now. Mark believes me and has given me his full support and so has Seb and Stuart…"

"So, I am the last to know?" I demanded angrily.

"No, it's not like that."

"How do I believe you, Jeremy, when you have lied to me?" I asked.

"I am telling you the truth," he stated sincerely.

"Now, when you have been found out, now you tell me. Why didn't you just tell me what had happened? If it is all innocent, why all the lies and deceit?" I pressed.

"I wanted her to stop, I thought that if I held out long enough she'd go back to London and never bother me again." He replied. "I can go and get Sebastian; he'll tell you that I am not lying, not on this."

"I need a drink," I said and walked out to the kitchen. I pulled a bottle of white wine from the fridge and put it on the table, lifting a glass from the dishwasher; I poured a glass of wine into it and drank it dry.

"I'm sorry, love, I should have told you. I should have trusted that you would understand."

"Yes, you should have," I agreed and sat at the table. Gripping the empty glass in my shaking fingers, afraid to let it go. "I can't believe that after all we have been through, you would allow this, this tart to come between us."

"It was out of my control," he said as he sat at the table. "I wanted to get control back and then I would be ready to talk to you."

"If you had come to me at the beginning, instead of making me feel you wanted to leave me, I would have…"

"No, you wouldn't, because you don't think you deserve to be happy or that you deserve to have me." He sighed loudly. "Let's face it, love, even after knowing that you hold the key to my heart, that I could never love another the way that I love you, you still think that it will be over one day. For you, there is no forever."

"That's not true," I frowned. "The thought of her touching you, it, it makes me feel sick."

"Makes me feel sick too, sweetheart," he sighed as he reached over to me, I pulled my hands back, out of his reach. He looked up from his quivering fingers and gazed into my eyes. He looked so hurt, so alone, so stupid and naïve. Rage filtered through my body, why did he have to be so bloody gullible?

I stood from the table and walked to the sink. The glass slipped through my fingers and hit the side of the sink before smashing into thousands of pieces over the floor.

"Don't move," he told me, "you have nothing on your feet." He raced towards me and began picking up the shards of glass around my toes. Sniffing as he did so, was he crying? Had I upset him that much? I tried to move. "Stand still," he ordered.

"I need the loo," I frowned and stepped over him, right on top of a piece of glass, "Ouch!" I hissed and began hobbling.

"Bloody hell, love, I told you to stand still."

"And I told you I need a wee," I retorted and hobbled to the toilet leaving a trail of blood behind me.

I cried as I peed, I truly cried, not just because I felt stupid and pathetic, not just because Jeremy was breaking my heart again, but on top of all of that, my sodding foot was killing me.

After flushing I sat on the toilet and pulled my foot up onto my knee so that I could see it. The door opened,

"Are you alright?" he asked.

"What do you think?" I sniffed.

"Let me see," he said softly, running the tap in the sink, he used the water to wash the blood from the bottom of my foot, he flashed his incredible eyes up to me and my heart skipped a beat. "I always seem to be rescuing you when you have hurt this foot." He smiled slightly.

"That's because when I am around you, bad things happen," I retorted.

"So, Harrison is bad, our wedding was bad…?"

"No, it was all amazing until Harrison got sick and you… well, this."

A sharp pain shot through my heel as Jeremy tugged on the glass, "That's it, got it." He said examining the glass between his finger and thumb. "I have to wash it again to make sure the glass is all out." He explained before rinsing my foot again. "Let me get you a plaster, stay there." He ordered and left me sat on the loo. Only I could take a septic situation and turn it into a drama with me ending up the victim. He returned with a Mr Bump plaster and stuck it to my heel, resting his hand on my foot he gazed into my eyes. "I am so sorry, my love," he muttered, his blue eyes filled with tears, "these past few weeks have been hell. I haven't had an affair, but I feel just as guilty." A tear dripped from his cheek and splashed on the back of his hand. "If I lost you, my life would be over."

"We'll sort something out," I promised and pushed my fingers over his ear, he caught my hand and pressed his tear sodden lips to the centre of my palm, kissing it softly before letting my hand go and standing.

He helped me as I hobbled to the living room,

"I'll mop this blood up," he said as I sat on the sofa.

I could see him washing the tiled hall floor with mop and I could smell the floral disinfectant. I waited for him to come back into the lounge and just as he stepped one foot in, the doorbell rang.

"That's probably Seb," he said.

"Mr Jeremy Buxton?" a male voice said.

"Yes," Jeremy replied.

"Can we come in?"

"Of course," he answered. Two men dressed in suits entered the living room, both looked at me, "My wife cut her foot on some glass, you'll have to excuse her for not standing." He explained.

"Mrs Buxton," one of the men said. "Are you okay?"

"Yes, who are you?" I asked.

"Oh, I am DCI Nick Challis and this is DCI Daniel Hollins." He answered. Challis literally looked like he had come from the seventies with his large over coat and heavy looking moustache. Hollins looked twenty-five, if that, he had sandy coloured hair and grey, unfeeling eyes.

"Police?" I questioned, "What's going on?"

"A complaint has been made against Mr Buxton." He answered.

"What sort of a complaint?" Jeremy asked, as the colour was already draining from his face.

"Miss Natasha Mason has made an allegation against you, sir," the other officer explained. "We need you to come in for questioning."

"What has she said?" Jeremy asked.

"I am sure you'd not want to discuss this in front of your wife." Hollins explained.

"Tell me or I am not going anywhere." He demanded.

"Miss Mason has made an allegation of sexual assault against you, sir?"

"What?" I stood, "Ouch," my foot. "You are joking," I frowned as pain shot through my foot.

"No, Mrs Buxton, we do not joke about this sort of allegation." Challis frowned.

"I don't understand," Jeremy said.

"Please get your coat, if you are innocent, then you have nothing to worry about." Challis stated sourly.

I picked up the phone, "Look at these messages, she has been harassing him for weeks." I said. "She's been threatening to ruin his life." I added. Hollins took the phone from my shaking hand.

"We'll look into it." He promised.

"Am I being arrested?" Jeremy asked.

"Not yet," Hollins shrugged.

"Jeremy?" I frowned with tears piercing my eyes, "What do I do?"

"I'll get it sorted out, okay?" he said lifting his car keys from the arm of the chair and putting them into his pocket.

I nodded and watched as he left.

That bitch, that bloody bitch.

I called my mother first and sobbed to her down the phone, then I waited, waited for the phone to ring so that Jeremy would come home. But the hours ticked by tediously slow and the sun began to set. I jumped up to the window at every car that passed the house. I had heard nothing and about to squeeze my sore foot into my boots to go to the station and demand that they let him go.

The front door opened and I jumped up and hobbled out to the hall, Stuart turned around,

"What's up, love?" he asked. I told him everything, about how I had to go and get his phone and whilst driving home, I saw him in his car with her. I told him about the argument we had had and then about the police carting him off like a criminal. Stuart seemed as shocked as me.

"I am sorry I didn't tell you what was going on, but they'll believe him, they have to."

"This will ruin his life," I sniffed and wiped away a few escaped tears.

"Shall I go down there?" he asked.

"I doubt they'll let you in," I sighed. His phone began to ring in his pocket.

"Hello?" he said. "What, where are you?" he looked at me. "Does Jez have his keys?" he asked me, I nodded. "Jez has got them mate, sorry."

"Is that Seb?" I asked, he nodded, "tell him what happened."

"Yes, Jez has been arrested for sexual assault on that slapper."

"No way!" I heard Seb yell, "Get me out of this fucking car now."

"I would, but Jez has the keys."

"What car?" I frowned.

"Jeremy's, it seems Seb was in the car the whole time recording everything, if she is claiming this happened today, she has screwed up, because Seb caught the whole meeting on camera."

I lifted the phone, "I am calling the station, they'll have to believe him now."

"What if it doesn't work?"

"You will be driving me to Blandford, I am going to confront that bitch."

Sixteen

Jeremy

I'd be lying if I said I wasn't scared, I was absolutely shitting myself. This was how she would ruin my life, take everything away. She planned to put me away and the concept petrified me. All I kept thinking about as they drove me to the new police station in Poole was how I would cope if they didn't believe me.

My father would most certainly disown me and I knew Kelsey would definitely leave me now. The police always seemed to believe the woman's side of the story; it was rare that a man actually got acquitted when he had done nothing wrong. How many men actually came forward with sexual harassment allegations against women? I hadn't heard of any, so if they had, it was kept out of the media and the press. It would make them look weak and pathetic and that was if anyone believed them at all.

DCI Hollins opened the back door and waited for me to get out. The sun was beginning to set and the cool wind blew around my neck as I walked with him at my side to a dark blue door. I was then led down a long, dark corridor and sat in a small room behind a table. To the left of the table there was a recording device of some sort and to the right I could see scribbles from others who had sat there before. I could see a small camera in the top corner behind the door and wondered if they were just standing in a room watching me as I fell to pieces.

After a long while the door opened and DCI's Challis and Hollins entered carrying paper cups of steaming coffee. They placed one on the table in front of me, he had put milk in it and I considered drinking it even though I knew it would make me sick, maybe they would let me go if I was puking all over the place.

"Is it too strong for you?" Hollins asked.

"I can't drink milk," I muttered nervously, "I'm lactose intolerant."

"Are you sure?" Challis asked.

"Yes, I even ended up in Bournemouth hospital on the day of my wedding because of cream put into a curry, I love curry, but really, who puts cream in a curry?" I replied, my mouth was running away through nerves. *Shut up you pleb!*

Hollins looked at Challis as he pulled the coffee away from me. "Sorry about that." Hollins said.

"Right, this isn't a formal interview, we just want to ask a few questions, okay?" I nodded. "And would you prefer if we call you Mr Buxton or is Jeremy alright?"

"Jeremy is fine," I answered and shifted in my seat.

They asked how I came to know Natasha and I briefly explained to them about the contracts for work and how we had shared dinners. How I received the first emails and what they said.

"Did you tell anyone?"

"Yes, my friend, Stuart."

"Stuart?"

"Stuart Lashmar, he lives at our house, our lodger and friend," I elaborated.

"And what did he tell you to do?"

"Tell my boss and tell my wife," I answered.

"But you didn't, this has supposedly gone on for a couple of weeks and you never told anyone that could stop it, right?" Challis groaned.

"No, I didn't want to lose my wife or my job and as Natasha said, she gave me a little while longer to decide."

"So, it was just messages and texts, a phone call or two, nothing physical?" Hollins checked.

I fidgeted in my seat again, "She uh, she touched me." I frowned.

"Excuse me?" Hollins frowned.

"On the Friday she told me what she wanted from me, she grabbed my penis through my clothes and rubbed it until I, I..." They looked at each other and then back at me, "Look, she masturbated me through my clothes and then got out of my car laughing at what she did. The woman is deranged, I promise you.

She has a screw or two loose." Sweat had formed on my forehead and my tie felt tight, I pulled at it to loosen it slightly.

"And while she uh… masturbated you, did you touch her?" Hollins asked.

"No, never. I wasn't attracted to her. I am still not attracted to her." I affirmed adamantly.

"But she is beautiful," He queried.

"Yes, to the eye she is, but I look a bit deeper than what's on the face, she is extremely beautiful, but she is cold and has an ugly heart."

"Some might say that you are bitter towards her because she wasn't interested in you." Challis stated.

"Have you read the messages?" I asked.

"Yes, okay. We need a little more information." He grumbled. "Have you ever attacked anyone?"

"Attacked?"

"Hit, had a fight with, been aggressive with someone?" Challis elaborated.

"I wouldn't say I attacked someone. I thumped someone in the face, Kyle Rogers. He is my wife's ex and he grabbed her while she was pregnant. He wouldn't let her go, so I made him." I replied and sat up in my seat. "I was arrested and locked up for the night. He dropped the charges a few weeks later and that was the end of it."

"Mmm, and you have never intentionally hurt a girl or…"

"Never," I asserted. "What did she say I did to her?"

"You tell us," Challis smirked.

"I didn't touch her. I have never touched her at any of our meetings, she touched me, not the other way around." I insisted.

"Well, she is claiming that you, uh, you groped her in your car and pushed your hand into her underwear." Hollins explained.

"In my car?"

"Yes," he nodded.

"When?" I asked.

"A couple of hours ago," Hollins affirmed.

"Today?" I double checked.

"Yes," Challis nodded firmly.

"Then I can prove she is lying," I stated, I almost smiled but though it would look complacent and at that moment, I was anything but. "My cousin, who works with me at The Press, is currently locked in the boot of my car with a Dictaphone and a video camera. He recorded the whole meeting. I told her that her plan had failed, that everyone knew the truth and then I drove her back to the Crown hotel."

"Are you sure he is still in your car?"

"I have the only key to my car here," I pulled them from my pocket and put them on the table. "My spare is at my family home, Glenwood in Canterbury." I replied feeling slightly more confident. "She is lying and I have proof. She even admitted why she made up the affair."

Challis lifted my keys and stood, "We'll go and get your cousin out of your boot."

"Okay," I nodded, "I'll just wait here then, shall I?"

"We won't be long," Challis added.

"I'll get you some black tea bought in," Hollins said and left.

I am not completely sure, but I felt their attitudes towards me changed. I only hoped Seb's recoding proved I was telling the truth and that Natasha was lying through her whitened teeth.

A female police officer bought in a cup of tea and I asked if I could at least call my wife and tell her that I am okay.

"Not yet," she replied and closed the door behind her.

My backside began to ache from sitting for so long. I felt sick and realized it was probably because I hadn't eaten properly in a few days. I sipped the tea, it was so strong, it seemed to stick to the back of my throat, but at least it was warm.

I needed to know that Kelsey was alright, that she wanted me at the end of it. I am not too proud to admit that the thought of losing her crippled me. The pain that shot through my heart was so ferocious; it almost bought me to tears. I only hoped she would listen to Seb and Stuart, that she'd listen to the recordings to confirm that I never did anything with Natasha and had no intention of touching her either.

An hour had passed, or so I thought, and I still hadn't heard if I was facing a prison term for standing up to a callous, psychotic bitch. I sat wishing that I had never agreed to have those stupid dinners with her in the first place. In fact, I wished I had never met her.

It astounded me how someone could cause me to lose all of my respect in a matter of moments. From that first message at work I should have just told Kelsey and perhaps it might not have come to this, me sitting in a police interview room waiting to find out what lie ahead for me.

When the female officer returned with another cup of tea, I asked if I could use the bathroom.

"I'll have to ask," she stated and left. When the door opened again, I thought it was her. DCI Hollins smiled slightly as he entered the room.

"Was he still there?" I asked keenly.

"He was," he replied. "Sorry we took so long; the recordings had to be saved onto discs so that we can use them in court."

"In court?" I frowned, shit, they were taking me to court.

"Sorry, Jeremy, I meant to tell you, you can go. We have arrested Natasha Mason, she has been charged with wasting police time and she is possibly looking at going to court for it."

"Seriously?" I smiled feeling instantly better.

"Yes," he held out his hand for me to shake. "Thanks for coming in, Jeremy; Sargent Shaw is going to give you a lift home."

"Thank you," I smiled.

"If you want to add to the charges, I would be more than happy to take a statement from you." He added as I approached the door.

He walked towards me holding out a card. "I'll think about it, but to be perfectly honest, I just want her out of my life." I admitted taking his card.

"Call me if you want to make a statement."

"Would I have a good case?" I asked.

"If it were me, I would have her charged, at least it would show her that you meant no." he asserted.

I nodded. "I'll give it some thought." I promised and left.

Sargent Shaw turned out to be the officer who had bought me tea, she only looked about twenty two, to think she was already ranking in the police force, was pretty impressive. She asked me about London and Eton as we rode home, I didn't want to make light chit chat, but it eased my nerves.

I got out of the car and thanked her before walking down my drive, both anxious and excited to see my wife and child, but so relieved to be finally free of Natasha Mason. I felt taller, my lungs filled with the cool evening air, the dark blue velvet sky twinkled with stars and before I opened the door, I took another clean breath of fresh air, blowing it out in an icy cloud.

My excitement was short lived though; Kelsey and Sebastian were yelling at each other and I caught the full force of it as I walked into the living room. She was sat on the couch and he was perched on the arm of the chair.

"Maybe if you actually talked to him instead of throwing orders and tantrums to get your own way, you might have picked up that he wasn't happy. He is bloody miserable, Kelsey, don't you see that, don't you see what you are doing to him?" Seb demanded.

"Obviously not, but he doesn't tell me anything, in fact, I think you and Jude know more about what's going on in his head than I do," Kelsey ranted.

"Look, you two, calm down," Stuart reasoned. None of them had noticed I was standing there like a complete and utter pleb. "Sebastian, Jeremy is a full grown adult, a husband and father, if he hasn't got the balls to tell Kelsey everything that is going on in his head, then it has nothing to do with anyone but them."

"All I am trying to say is if she gave him room to breathe, to take the reins once in a while, she would see that he is more than capable of handling everything." Seb sighed and turned his head towards me. "Oh," he frowned, his cheeks glowed red. "You're back, where is your stripy uniform?"

"I wasn't even arrested," I scowled. "What's going on?"

"Nothing," Kelsey glowered at Seb. "What did they say?"

"They said they have charged Natasha for wasting police time and asked me if I want to press charges against her," I replied.

"Please tell me you are," Seb said standing from the arm of the chair.

"I don't know, I told them I'd think about it." I shrugged.

"What's to think about?" Stuart asked, "She almost ruined your life."

"Well, maybe I just want it all over and done with." I looked at Kelsey, she rolled her eyes and left the room. "What's going on with you two?"

"She has blamed everything on you, calling you weak and gullible. I just put her in her place." He muttered. "I am just sticking up for you, cuz, that's all."

I didn't like to hear that she blamed me, but I suppose I was expecting it, she'd never blame Natasha, would she? "Thanks, but I can take care of myself." I grumbled.

"Sure you can, cuz, that's why I was locked in your boot for five fucking hours." Seb snapped.

"I know, sorry, okay? I am sorry I dragged you into this mess." I held out my hand. "Thank you, Sebastian, you saved my arse."

He smiled slightly and shook my hand adding, "Again!"

"I'll give you a lift home if you want," Stuart offered, "Kelsey and Jez can talk then."

"Good idea, I am getting chill blains from frosty knickers," Seb joked just as Kelsey came back into the room. Stuart smirked and turned away so she couldn't see him. "I'm going home, Kelse, aside from the fact that you hate my guts, will you still come tomorrow night?"

She flashed her eyes at me, "I might," she shrugged and handed me a cup of black tea. "I'll try and thaw my knickers out first though." She added.

"Don't do that on my account," he grinned. "You love me really."

"Mmm," she nodded and smiled wryly, "like a hole in the head."

As they left I sat on the couch nursing my tea. She hovered, moved around the room, looked out of the window and sighed so many times, I lost count. "No," I stated. She turned to face me. "No," I said again. "I don't blame you for any of this. This is completely my fault and you should take no notice of my cousin, he is all mouth and no action."

"But a lot of what he said is true." She said and turned to face me, crossing her arms over her chest and leaning against the windowsill. "You don't tell me anything and I suppose there is only one reason for that, you don't trust me anymore."

"I do, I trust you with my life, I just, I can't…"

"You can't talk to me, you never have, not really. Everything I know about you has either come from someone else or I have had to pry it out of you."

"That's not true," I protested.

She stared before sighing again, "It is true. Look at tonight, look at what happened and how out of control that got. That is not healthy or normal at all. If you had trusted me enough from the start, none of this would have happened."

"I do trust you." I insisted.

"Well, it doesn't feel like it. You trusted Stuart and Sebastian, you even trusted Mark enough to tell him, but me, I came last. Once again I am the last to know." She walked towards the door, "According to Seb, the whole office knows and I am a laughing stock."

"No, no you're not." I frowned. "She sent e-mails to them all. I had nothing to do with it."

She stared for a while, I couldn't read her thoughts, her eyes showed me nothing, "So, what happens now? Are you going to have her charged?"

"I should do, but that would mean a court case and I don't want to see her ever again."

"If they have charged her, you may not have a choice." She stated and crossed the room, "I'll cook you something to eat."

"I'm not hungry," I grumbled.

"Crap, you must be." She called over her shoulder and left the room.

She stayed out in the kitchen for ages, when I went out to check on her, I could see she was crying over a pan of vegetable soup. I put my cup on the table and she straightened her back.

"I'm so sorry, Kelsey, I never meant for any of this to happen and I certainly didn't want to upset you like this."

"I'm just tired," she croaked. I moved in behind her and pushed her blonde hair away from her shoulder, exposing her neck. Wrapping my arms around her, I placed my lips on her neck and kissed her softly. She pressed her back into me, breathing in deeply, but as if something had hit her, she stiffened and moved forward, shrugging my lips off her shoulder. "Do you want bread with your soup?"

"Uh, no," I frowned and stepped back from her. "I told you, I am not hungry."

"Well, I have cooked it now."

"Give it to Stuart, I am going to take a shower." I added sourly and left her in the kitchen.

I ran up the stairs and into the bathroom, Kelsey was already blaming me for everything and I just wondered now, how much longer she would tolerate me in her life.

Seventeen

Kelsey

Why didn't I believe my husband? Even after all of the proof and witnesses, a small part of me doubted the truth. I was so angry at Sebastian and their stupid plan if I am honest. It could have gone so wrong and Jeremy could have been looking at being locked up for a very long time. I believed nothing happened between them, but a small part of me also believed that he wanted something to happen, that somewhere in his wild imagination, he had thought about her that way.

When the officers returned and unlocked the boot, Sebastian jumped out, looking slightly flushed, not just from the heat in the boot, but also anger. I could see it in his wild eyes. They looked like they were on fire, a roaring fire and who was on the receiving end of his wrath? Me!

"If you knew he was innocent you should have told me," I snapped.

"Oh yeah, 'cos you are all full of understanding," he countered. "You would rather think that of him than believe he actually loves you." He barked.

"Well, if he had told me, then none of this would have happened and she would be gone, but no. In true Jeremy style, he held it all in, making my life hell in the process."

"Your life hell?" he demanded, it shocked me. "Maybe if you actually talked to him instead of throwing orders and tantrums to get your own way, you might have picked up that he wasn't happy. He is bloody miserable, Kelsey, don't you see that, don't you see what you are doing to him?" Seb asked.

I frowned and stiffened at his accusation, I was smothering him. "Obviously not, but he doesn't tell me anything, in fact, I think you and Jude know more about what's going on in his head than I do," Kelsey ranted.

"Come on you two, please calm down," Stuart reasoned. I wanted to leave, to go somewhere, away from Seb and his accusations, away from Stuart and his glaring eyes. I didn't want to admit what a self-centred bitch I had become. Hearing it from Seb meant that others had seen how I was. *Oh ground, swallow me now!*

He went on and I shouted back, I would not let him get the better of me and the more he kept on, the more I hit back. I didn't even hear the door or notice my husband standing there, just watching us.

I had to get out of that room and when Jeremy said he would rather drop it all than press charges against Natasha, my fears were realized, he must have felt something for her. He could say he didn't, but I knew him, I knew he would never want to hurt someone on purpose, even if they had wronged him. Jeremy was a carer, he cared about others and their feelings, but more importantly, he cared about what others thought about him. This wasn't a pride thing, Jeremy didn't want to upset Natasha.

I made tea in the kitchen allowing the kettle to drown out the noise of Seb and Jeremy talking. My hands shook and I felt so sick, why was I so scared? He had come home to me, he was there and he was finally telling the truth.

After the others had gone, we could talk, but I didn't want to, I was tired and had a head ache. I wanted the day to be over and our lives to get back to normal, but after this, I wondered if we would ever have a normal life again.

He said he wasn't hungry, but he had to be, he'd obviously not eaten all day, playing Magnum PI must have worn him out. I decided that soup might help him, it wasn't a meal as such, but something in his stomach.

The house seemed so quiet and I had to phone my mother to let her know Jeremy was home so that she could bring Harrison back, while I thought about it, Jeremy put his cup on the table, snapping me back.

"I'm so sorry, Kelsey, I never meant for any of this to happen and I certainly didn't want to upset you like this." He said from behind.

"I'm just tired," I lied. Within moments he folded his arms around my waist, pressing his lips to my neck. I pushed against him, enjoying his embrace as I always had. But I couldn't just forget all that had happened, I moved forward, away from his body until his arms dropped and his lips left my skin. *Nice try, Jeremy Buxton, but you have a lot of sucking up to do!*

Of course he threw a major tantrum and left me cooking soup for Mr Nobody again. I was a bitch, I was born a bitch. I put up defences and every time I let them down, I got hurt. Not this time, no way. I would not let this destroy me, I was tough, as hard as nails and if Jeremy didn't trust me enough to tell me what was going on, then I suppose that said everything and it left me wondering if he trusted me over anything.

I was not going to spend the rest of my married life walking on egg shells. I had done nothing wrong, technically neither had Jeremy, but he just had to tell me the truth from the start. He had a lesson he needed to learn, trust had to be earned and I had a few ideas of how he could earn that trust again.

Mum dropped Harrison off, it was after nine by the time I got him to bed and as she left, Stuart returned. He had made plans with Elliot and I ironed his shirt for him so that they could go out clubbing in town.

"Are you sure you are alright?" Stuart asked. I looked at the living room door, to where Jeremy had sat most of the evening, sulking.

"Yes," I answered. "So, how are things with Elliot?" I asked, changing the subject.

"He's a great guy. He's just a bit up tight." He shrugged.

"You know he has never been with anyone before, right?"

"I guessed that, I am working on him." He smiled and sipped his beer. "I like his naiveté, its endearing, he is funny and cute and sweet but…"

"He's not Luke, he'll never be Luke and if you are going to get over Luke, then you need to let him go." I frowned and handed him his blue shirt.

"Why is love so sodding complicated?" he groaned.

"Loving someone is easy, it's trusting them that's tricky." I sighed.

"You're right, if love was all plain sailing, it would be as bland as a Korma." He smiled. The door knocked. "Bugger, that's him now." He began to panic, "Tell him I won't be long."

I took his arm as he passed me, "Take a breath," I smiled and kissed his cheek.

"Thanks, babes." He grinned and left the kitchen. Jeremy let Elliot in as I put away the ironing board.

"Hi," he said sheepishly from the door.

"Hi, he said he won't be long." I replied.

"Thanks," he smiled slightly.

"Have a seat," I said, "I will make us a coffee."

He nodded and sat at the table, "I am telling him tonight," he muttered.

"Telling him?" I frowned.

"That I am in love with him." he affirmed.

"Do you want my advice?" I asked. He nodded. "Don't tell him yet, he is besotted with you, but Luke hurt him badly and it may scare him off if you start throwing out the 'L' word just yet."

"Okay, so, shall I just let him know I like him then?"

"Go for it." I smiled.

"Hello, gorgeous," Stuart grinned from the door. Elliot's face and eyes lit up. "Are you ready?"

"Yes," Elliot smiled crookedly and stood from the table. "See you tomorrow, Kelsey, Stuart is taking me to your cousin's house for the party."

"Great, I'll see you then." I nodded.

They yelled goodbye to Jeremy, he murmured something back to them and the door slammed. I went to the living room, he flashed his incredible eyes at me and my heart melted. I had to be firm though.

"I am going to take a bath, when I come out, I suggest you be in bed waiting for me." I stated firmly.

"What?"

"You heard me," I replied.

"How long will you be?"

"Not long." I shrugged and hurried upstairs.

After a short bath, with the towel wrapped around my body I headed to our bedroom, Jeremy was in bed, like I had instructed, lying against the headboard with his arms folded across his chest. God, I loved that chest.

"Nice bath?" he asked.

"Yes, thank you." I nodded and sat on the bed. "So, I have decided that I want to put this thing behind us, but there are few things you need to do to make it up to me."

"Make it up to you, I've done nothing wrong?"

"If you think that, then there is more wrong than I first thought."

"Fine, so, how can I make it up to you? What would you like me to do? Beg?"

"No, not beg, something like, a full body massage, to begin with." I answered modestly. I turned to face him, "It's not sex, I don't want sex with you at the moment, but I do want you to show me how you love me without making love to me."

"Okay," he nodded. Suddenly looking so young, he tried not to smile as he pushed the bed covers off. "I'll get the oil."

I opened the towel, keeping it against my back and laid face down on the bed, with the towel draped over my naked body, waiting for him to return. It was going to be hard on us both, but I needed to know that we were more than sex. You'd think after two and a half years of marriage I would know that already, but recently it seemed Jeremy thought the only way to show me how much he loved me was with sex, this had to change.

He returned to the room and hovered by the door, "What's wrong?" I asked.

"Nothing, but, um, I am going to have to move that towel."

"Okay," I shrugged.

I felt him kneel on the bed and slowly pull the towel from my damp body. As soon as the cool air hit my skin, I covered in goose bumps. I felt a small drop of oil drip in the middle of my back, he sat over my legs, the warmth of his legs set my senses alight, this was not going to be easy. His warm hands began smoothing the oil over my back in small, firm yet gentle strokes, up over my shoulders and down the back of my arms.

Every sumptuous stroke made my core warm, smouldering away, like a burning lamp, flickering in a dark and dense night. As the strokes intensified, my lamp burned brighter and brighter, not having sex with him was going to be torture. I had to be strong, I had to show him that I meant business.

But his hands were creating magic, lighting up my soul and melting the ice around my heart. Jeremy was slowly working his way back to an early forgiveness. I forgot myself and allowed a moan to escape my lips. My eyes snapped open and I looked up to him, he wore a small, arrogant grin on his face, the ice hardened just as his crutch hardened against my backside, I would not give in, not matter how much my body screamed at me to be satisfied.

"Shall I do your legs now?" he asked.

"Yes," I replied. I felt him slide down to my ankles, followed by more oil splashing on my claves. "Shit," he snapped. "Sorry. I just got oil all over the sheets."

"It'll wash out," I shrugged.

His long fingers began rubbing my calf muscles, which actually hurt. You could tell I had started wearing heeled shoes again. As his fingers slowly found their way up my legs, I wanted to part them so that he could go higher and higher. It took everything I had in me to stop my thighs from opening, especially when his slick fingers slid between them just below my backside. Before I allowed another traitorous moan to escape, he stopped and moved his hands back down to my ankles.

"Shall I do your front now?" he asked. I knew this was not going to be easy, the back was hard enough.

"No," I frowned and moved up to my knees. I turned and watched as he stood. I climbed off the bed. "I'm tired." I lifted my night dress and pulled it over my head. I frowned at him standing there slightly bewildered, with oil soaked hands and a huge hard-on held snug inside his boxer shorts. Tough, he had to learn to trust me and know that I would not put up with lies, ever.

"Right, well I'll go and wash my hands then." He huffed and left the room.

I climbed into bed and waited for him to come back into the room. He was a while, but when he returned, he had the same sour look on his face. He climbed into bed without saying a word.

Sighing loudly he turned to me, "Can I at least get a kiss goodnight?" he asked sharply.

"Yes," I nodded and allowed him to peck my lips. I grabbed at the tuft of hair on his neck, just to hold his lips against mine a little while longer, *'Kelsey, be strong!'* I let him go, he pulled his face back and gazed into my yes.

"What is it going to take to convince you of how sorry I am?" he asked.

"Time," I replied. He nodded and turned away from me.

He switched off the light on his side as I slid down the bed and pulled the covers over my shoulders.

It took hours for me to fall asleep, I don't think I was alone though, Jeremy seemed to toss and turn as well. I woke when he climbed out of bed, the room was still dark and the cold of the house hurt my lungs. We were told not to run the heating at night as it could upset Harrison's breathing, but the house felt so cold. I climbed from the bed, pulled on my robe and hurried down the stairs to put the heating on.

Jeremey was in the kitchen, sat at the table in his dark blue robe. His hair was a mess on his head and he needed a shave. He had a steaming cup of tea in front of him. Silently I walked towards the kettle to make a drink,

"There is tea in the pot." He murmured.

"Oh, thanks," I said. My body felt amazing and I could still smell the oil as I moved around the kitchen. I glanced at the clock, it was almost seven, bloody Saturday and neither of us could sleep.

"I have to help Jude and Seb today, they have a lot to do for tonight." He explained as I sat at the table.

"Okay, what are we getting them?"

"They don't want anything," he frowned, "but I suppose you could get them a bottle of bubbly today, if you don't mind."

"I don't mind, it's definitely not fancy dress is it?"

"No, I told him I wouldn't go if it was." He replied.

"Thank God for that," I sighed and sipped my tea.

We sat in silence for a while, until he stood and announced he was going for a shower. This was fine, in a few days it would be all over with and we could get back to normal.

I stayed downstairs until I heard Harrison cry. By the time I got up to his room, Jeremy had him in his arms, cuddling him so tightly, I held back at the door.

"Daddy loves you so much," he croaked. "I can't believe how close I came to losing you."

"Daddy, cry," Harrison, said.

"No, I'm not," Jeremy sniffed. "You be a good boy for Mummy today, okay?"

"Okay," he replied. I stepped into the room.

"It's a bit early to go yet," I frowned.

"I have a few things to do first," he said. More lies? "No, nothing like that, just trust me, okay? Please?" I nodded. He walked towards me and kissed me tenderly. He handed Harrison to me and his facial expression scared me, "I'll be at the Manor around three, I have to go into the office to see Mark, he has texted for me to go in. I can show you if you don't believe me."

"I believe you, what does he want?"

"They probably heard about what happened last night and knowing my luck, he is going to sack me. I don't expect it's a good image for the company, the Copy Editor pressing charges against someone who would have bought a lot of money into the company."

"Are you pressing charges then?"

"I don't know yet," he frowned.

"Well, if he sacks you, we will take him to a tribunal." I stated sternly.

"Okay," he nodded and kissed my lips again, "I love you." He added. He kissed Harrison's head and left before I could say it back.

I dressed Harrison after his breakfast and got ready to leave the house to go shopping. We needed a card at the very least. I also wanted to get something to take. I didn't want to show up empty handed. So we headed to the supermarket and did the grocery shop at the same time.

On the way to the car I received a text message, then another. I searched my bag for my phone and when I pulled it out, it was a number I didn't know. I shoved my phone back into my bag and forgot about it until much later that day.

Jeremy called at two thirty to say he was not fired for sticking up for himself, but the company were holding their own investigation as it seemed her father was none too pleased and wanted all of the facts. He said he would see me at the party as he had arranged, they were only just setting up the marquee in the back garden.

After dinner, I changed into a red dress with a scooped back and black knee high boots, they weren't exactly flat, but they were better than the heeled shoes I had worn all week. I pinned up my hair allowing a few wisps to fall freely around my shoulders and dabbed on a little make up with my new red lipstick, I felt a million dollars.

For about the first hour of the evening we had nothing but children knocking the door for treats. Harrison loved it, he held the bowl and smiled as they took handfuls of sweets.

Just after six the door opened followed by Elliot and Stuart coming in.

"You look bloody lovely, Kelse," he gushed pecking my cheek.

"Thank you," I smiled smoothing my dress down.

"How are things?" he asked.

"Tense," I answered.

"Where is Jez?"

"He's already there, I am just getting Harrison ready to go to my mum's and then I will drive over there. Need a lift?"

"If you don't mind," he shrugged.

"Of course not, is this the first time you have been home since last night?" I asked.

"Yes, Elliot let me kip on his couch to give you two some much needed space." He explained. I grinned knowingly and looked at a red faced Elliot. "Nothing like that, crikey, you have a one tracked mind, girl.

"I didn't say a word." I shrugged.

"No, you didn't have to," He chuckled. "I just need to change and I am ready."

"I'll pack Harrison's bag." I said and left them in the kitchen. I forgot to take his back pack with me and turned to see them kissing, I felt like I was intruding, so hurried out of the kitchen leaving them to it.

I envied them in a way, starting a new relationship was both exciting and nerve wracking. I remembered the first night I met Jeremy at a party at the Manor and tonight we were going to be at a party there again. Jude and Seb were engaged and back then on that night, she could have only dreamed of being his forever. I just wanted someone to love me as much as I loved them, I thought I had found it, but the weeks leading up to this night weighed heavy on my heart and that scared me.

After dropping Harrison off at my Mum's we drove out to Winterborne Kingston to Buxton Manor. As we drove the long and winding roads to north Dorset, the smoky air of the woods and nearby houses burning fires, filled the car. Winter was almost here and I couldn't wait to snuggle up in the living room with Jeremy and Harrison on Sunday afternoons and watch movies. I refused to allow the 'What ifs?' to plague me at that moment, I just wanted normal.

The party was in full swing when we arrived. I parked on the gravel driveway and gazed up at the huge light brick house. Music thumped through the windows and decorations of ghosts and ghouls were everywhere I looked. Stuart linked his arms with me and Elliot and we walked in together.

The grand hall was packed, I scoped the room and saw Jude rushing over,

"Here she is," she announced loudly, "my maid of honour." She hugged me and pecked my cheek. I handed her the bottle bag and card I had got for them. "Thank you, but we said no gifts." She frowned; I gave her a stern look. "Sorry, its lovely, thank you." She smiled. "Are you okay?" she asked.

"Yes I am fine, where is Jeremy?"

"Ooh, I should warn you, he's not very happy, Mark and Brian are holding a formal meeting with him on Monday, seems Mr Mason is looking to sue the company. To add insult to injury, Elle and Hermione are stuck at home babysitting your brother-in-law, he apparently is grounded for the rest of the half term break for smoking pot in their father's DB9."

"Shit, I better go and talk to him."

I found him slumped over a bottle of beer in the kitchen, head resting on his hand, looking sullen, but incredibly gorgeous at the same time. "Jeremy," I said. "Jude told me what happened with Mark, are you okay?"

He looked up and frowned, shook his head and sighed, "Nope."

"Do you think they'll sack you?" I asked.

He turned the corners of his mouth down, "I don't know, maybe. Did you get the bubbly?"

I nodded, "Yes, I gave it to Jude. Do you want to go home?" I asked.

"No, I am the best man," he sighed and stood, "we have to stay a while." He held out his hand, I placed my hand into his. "You look beautiful." He smiled, it made my cheeks warm.

"Thank you," I muttered as he squeezed my hand. My heart skipped a beat. *You might just get lucky tonight, Mr Buxton.* "So um, Julian is being a little turd again then."

"Yes, even I wasn't stupid enough to smoke in the DB9, he must have a death wish." He nodded. "There's always Christmas," he added.

"There is," I agreed, though I would not be going to Glenwood or anywhere, I wanted Christmas at home and if the Buxton family wanted to see us, they could come down to Dorset for a change.

I got a glass of lemon and lime soda water and sat beside him on the sofa in one of the many rooms. Revellers were everywhere and I couldn't even tell you where the hosts were. Jeremy left me to go to the toilet, his beer remained untouched, it seemed neither of us were in the partying mood.

Nicki and Felix arrived with Lou and Shawna and for a while, Jeremy perked up. Apparently Felix and Nicki had been there during the day to help set up also. It was good to see him and Jeremy talking and laughing again. I slipped away to use the loo and while I was in the bathroom, shut off from the noise and clatter, my phone buzzed again. I lifted it out of my bag, I now had seven messages from this number, so I opened the first. It was a picture of Jeremy having sex on a bed, the next message said the date, which was just before his wedding to Tara, then another and he was having sex with another girl.

'How much do you trust your husband now?' the message read.
'He has lied to you from the start.'

I felt so sick as vomit rushed to my throat, I threw up so violently it actually caused me pain. One of the pictures was the night of Felix's stag do when I was in Majorca with Nicki. How could he? He never mentioned any of these girls when I asked him. He promised me he hadn't cheated on any of his ex's and yet here he was, having sex with other women while he was supposed to be engaged to Tara, add me into that factor and some might have called him a slut.

I couldn't think straight, my hands shook and my blood boiled. I gazed at myself in the mirror, my eyes filled with tears, lies and more lies. Bullshit was everywhere I looked and I wanted answers.

I rinsed my mouth and ran to find him. Seb and Felix were joking with him, he laughed and looked over at me as my eyes filled with tears once again. The man I so totally and completely loved with every part of me, my heart and my soul, was a liar and what scared me more was the fact that he found it so easy to live with.

I had to get out of there. I shook my head and ran for the door. Pushing my way through the revellers, I could hear Jeremy calling after me, but I had to go.

"Kelsey?" Jude frowned.

"Sorry," I spluttered, "I have to go."

I slammed the front door closed behind me and ran for my car.

I started my car with a roar and sped out of the driveway, flicking stones up behind my car. I could see him on the front porch with Jude, the tears ran and I wiped them from my stinging eyes, how could he?

Jeremy

Eighteen

Sexual frustration is the worst thing to try and sleep with and this was the second time I had been left high and dry that week. I lay there listening to my wife as she slept so peacefully, how? I have no idea. The few hours leading up to bed time had been the worst in my life, facing a prison sentence for something I hadn't even done bore heavily on my mind. All I kept thinking about was what if they didn't believe me, or if her father offered them money to charge me instead?

He must have been upset, I know I would have been. His perfect, little princess was far from innocent. She proved herself to be the psycho I had thought she was, since that very first message, a dangerous psycho and I doubted very much that this would be the end of it. In fact, I would go as far as saying, she would come back with a vengeance, though I had no idea of what lengths she would go to destroy my life completely.

I received two text messages very early that morning. The first was from Sebastian asking if I could help him with the party and the second was from Mark, he wanted to talk about what had happened. I wondered how long it would have been before he found out. She probably called her father when she was arrested and he would have called either Brian or Mark and the thought of having to explain entrapping her into confessing what she did, using equipment from work didn't sit well.

I got up when the message came from Mark, I couldn't sleep once I knew my job could be on the line for defending myself. I wrapped my robe around my body and hurried down the stairs. I needed a pee and wished I had used the upstairs toilet, but didn't want to wake either Kelsey or Harrison. I know she was awake during the night, I doubted it was due to being sexually frustrated though. I tried very hard to turn her on, but I suppose her anger at me and all that had happened prevented that.

I made a pot of tea and heard the bed creak upstairs. I didn't realize it made so much noise and wondered if Stuart had ever heard us. When she entered the kitchen things still felt off, she had that look on her face, I couldn't blame her, but I didn't know how long it would be until things were back to normal for us or if they ever would get back to normal for us again.

She sighed while staring at her cup of tea. I couldn't make the situation better, so I went for a shower after telling her about having to help Seb. She didn't seem to be that bothered at all.

I dried my face after shaving and packed a bag so that I could change at the Manor before the party. I came out of our room as Harry started to cry. Lifting him from his bed I held him against my chest and kissed his cheek. He felt so warm in my arms and smelled so good.

"You sad, Daddy?" he said. For two and a half, his speech was pretty amazing.

"Daddy loves you very much," I said as my eyes filled with tears. "I can't believe how close I am to losing you, little man."

"Daddy, cry," he added and touched my cheek with his hand.

"No, I'm not," I sniffed. "You be a good boy for mummy today, okay?"

"Okay," he promised and hugged me again.

"It's a bit early to go yet," Kelsey said from the door, I turned to face her.

"I have a few things to do first." She frowned, of course, she didn't believe me. "No, nothing like that," I explained about Mark and she looked concerned. I told her not to worry and before leaving I pecked her lips.

It choked me up if I am honest; it literally felt like she was slipping through my fingers. Was I going to have to explain to her about everywhere I went and who I met? I started my car and reversed out of the drive.

The office car park was deserted, then I saw Mark's BMW parked near the rear door. I climbed out feeling slightly apprehensive and made my way inside. I knocked on the door to his office and he called out for me to come in.

"Are you alright?" he asked walking towards me. He looked so different in jeans a check shirt. I had never seen him in anything but a suit.

"I will be honest, Mark, I absolutely shit myself." I admitted. "I was sat in that room for almost four hours and all I could think about was that I could go down for nothing."

"Brian called me late last night after the Masons contacted him, he was furious that it had got this serious."

"Well, after meeting her yesterday she said she hoped I liked prison food, I honestly thought they were going to lock me up." Then I smiled. "Then they told me it was the time I had met her with Seb in my boot, he saved my arse, literally."

"He sure did." He then frowned, "Take a seat." I nodded and sat opposite him. "So uh, her father is kicking up a fuss. Saying how Brian and I let it get too out of hand. I have to know, Jeremy, when did it exactly change from her doing a little flirting to her being a stalking psycho?"

"That Friday you gave me the afternoon off, I showed you all the messages she sent me." I explained.

"Right, and the dinners?"

"Strictly business," I confirmed. "I am not, and never have been attracted to her. She was sort of, cocky, like, look at me, every guy wants me and because I didn't, I suppose she made it her goal to ruin me."

"Okay. Well, Brian has asked for a formal investigation, we have to take this seriously now the police have been involved. One, it will show the other team members that all client contact is to remain business only and two, it will show future customers that we have a professional, trust worthy staff."

"And, do you trust me, Mark?" I asked.

"I told you, I will back you up one hundred percent, if I didn't trust you I wouldn't. It's just Brian, because Mason is an absolute tosser, we have to do this properly. So there will be an investigation, Brian is coming down next Wednesday for a formal meeting with you and I. Mr Mason will be joining us too. He has instigated that he may actually sue the company if Natasha is cleared of the charges. With that being said, I hate to add this, but we have to suspend you, Jeremy, pending the outcome of the investigation."

"You have got to be joking," I frowned. "After everything that bitch has done to me, I am suspended. This is bollocks," I snapped and stood.

"You'll be paid, Jeremy, I have to go by the book."

"Yeah, whatever, mate. Cheers for, you know, having my back." I barked and left his office, slamming the door behind me.

I stopped by the river in Blandford before going to the Manor. I needed to clear my head. She had done it, she had all but destroyed my marriage and now I was losing my job. Natasha had won, she had done all she said she would and I hadn't laid a finger on her.

I texted Kelsey, telling her everything was alright, I didn't want to worry her, but as soon as I sent it, I realized I was lying to her again. What the fuck was wrong with me? Why couldn't I just be a bloody man and sort this all out once and for all?

I dialled the number on the card, DCI Hollins answered after only a few rings.

"Hello?"

"DCI Hollins, its Jeremy Buxton. I've decided I want to make a statement and have Natasha Mason charged."

"Alright, when would you like to do this?"

"Uh, do you work tomorrow?"

"I am working all weekend, I'll come to your house at around eleven and we'll get this sorted. I think you have made the right decision."

"Yeah, well, she can't go around trying to ruin someone's life and get away with it." I replied. "Thank you, I will see you tomorrow at eleven."

I arrived at the Manor just before twelve after pondering on how my life would have been so much easier if I had refused to work with Natasha in the first place. Kelsey was probably contemplating life without me, Mark and Brian were more than likely working out a way to sack me... no, no. I had to stop this and man up. I had to take the control back. Arranging to make a statement against her was a good start, Kelsey would see that.

First mission was to take Seb shopping, seriously the bloke didn't have a ruddy clue. The last party he had, I organised the food and considering this was meant to be an engagement party, they didn't even have a plate.

I ordered some platters to be made up by one of the supermarkets and then we hit the stores for the rest. I told Jude to get on with setting everything up while Seb and I got the food and alcohol.

When we got back to the Manor it started to resemble somewhere that was actually having a party. Nicki and Felix had arrived to lend a hand and I was relieved to see him, he chopped up the salads and prepared the sea food platter making it look professional. The DJ arrived and set up in the main hall and the bar staff arrived at six.

I changed while Jude and Seb were getting ready and waited for Kelsey to arrive. I chatted with Felix about everything that had gone on. He told how he had bumped into Kelsey at the supermarket and she asked him if I had ever cheated on any of my ex's. She already had doubts and my behaviour added to her fears. No wonder she was so ready to believe the worst. Felix and Nicki had to collect Louise and Shawna as arranged by Nicki, so they left to pick them up. I just sat and waited for my wife to arrive.

She found me slumped over a beer in the kitchen. I wasn't in a party mood and just wanted to go home. I felt a failure, to both her and our child. He deserved a better father than I was and she deserved a better husband. I think I was actually looking forward to seeing my siblings, so learning that Julian had been a prat during his half term holiday from school royally pissed me off.

She placed her hand on my back, the warmth felt good, "Jude told me what happened
with Mark, are you okay?"

I looked up frowning, shaking my head, I sighed loudly, "Nope."

"Do you think they'll sack you?" she asked.

"I don't know." I wanted to change the subject, I was so sick of thinking about it all of the time. "Did you get the bubbly?"

She nodded her head, "I gave it to Jude. Do you want to go home?" she then asked looking so concerned.

"No, I am the best man," I replied and stood, "we have to stay a while." I held out my hand and she took it. "You look beautiful," I stated squeezing her hand lightly.

"Thank you," she blushed slightly, her eyes twinkled in the lights of the room. "So um, Julian is being a little turd again then."

"Yes, even I wasn't stupid enough to smoke in the DB9, he must have a death wish." I nodded. "There's always Christmas," I added. A visit back to Canterbury could be what we needed.

We found a couch in one of the lounges and sat down watching everyone enjoy themselves. Felix and Nicki returned with Louise and Shawna and all I could think about was had she told them all what a prick I had been?

At least they managed to cheer me up a bit. I had missed Felix, since both of us had married, neither of us seemed to have any time for each other. Something I planned to change.

"So, have you told her?" Felix asked.

"Jude got there first," I replied and put my warm bottle of beer on the table. "We are going to talk tonight though, I am making sure of it."

"I tell Nicki everything, there's no point in hiding anything from her, women have this built in bullshit radar, I swear to God."

"Kelsey suspected I am sure, but she never seemed to ask me anything." I admitted. "I can't lose her, Felix, it will literally kill me."

"Then you have to be honest with her, protecting her by lying will not help. She's not a fragile flower, that girl is a bloody black belt and more than capable of handling the truth, even if it's not what she wants or needs to hear."

"I can't believe how naïve I was. Natasha has ruined my confidence, I know that much."

"What's this, Jezza Buxton admitting a piece of skirt knocked him off his high horse?"

I chuckled, "Yeah, scary thought, huh?"

"We need to have a man weekend, go paintballing, fishing, anything that says we're men and we can face anything."

I turned the corners of my mouth down, "Fishing?"

"Yes, can't be anything too vigorous, I am always knackered these days," he smiled.

"Work getting to be too much?" I asked.

"No, it's my insanely horny wife, seriously, I have to book time to sleep or take a leak." He laughed. I joined in his laughter, I never thought I'd hear Felix complain about having too much sex.

Someone entered the room, I looked over and saw Kelsey, she looked distressed as she frowned at me, I smiled nervously, she shook her head and hurried out. "Is she alright?" Felix asked.

"I don't know." I stood from the arm of the couch, "I'll be back in a bit." I hurried through the crowds, Jude was staring at the front door. "Where did she go?" I asked her.

"I think she's gone," she answered and raced towards the door. I joined her and watched as my wife sped out of the drive way roaring up the road. *Shit, what have I done now?*

"You have to go after her, Jez, she could crash in that state."

"I am. So glad I didn't drink yet tonight." I pulled my keys from my pocket, "I'll ring you later and let you know what happens, tell Seb I'm sorry."

"Sod that, just go," Jude insisted.

I headed back towards our house and prayed that whatever it was that upset her, I could make it right. My insides gnawed at each other, I'd had nothing to eat all day and my chest felt so tight, that I could hardly breathe.

Every bloody light turned red and kept me waiting; I swear it was on purpose, adding to my already rising anxiety. I had no idea of what or who had upset her. When she ran like this, all I could do was chase and I would chase her to the end of the world if I had to. The concept of facing life without her in it was unimaginable. I couldn't live without her, she was my air and I needed her to breathe.

I pulled onto the drive behind her car, thankful that she had the good sense to go home. I opened the front door,

"Kelsey," I called out. But I got nothing back. I ran through the dark house. The only light on I could see was coming from my office, then I heard the printer. "Kelsey, why did you leave?" I asked pushing open the door. She turned with tears streaming in mascara trailing down her face and handed me a print.

"I can't decide which one is my favourite," she croaked. I looked at the print. It was one of the pictures Natasha had of me. The printer spat out another, "I think it's this one." She held up the picture, it was the one where a girl, I don't know who, but she was naked and sat astride me on a couch and I had her nipple in my teeth. "It really beings out your eyes," she said through gritted teeth and threw it in my face.

"This was before us," I frowned.

"Well, this was taken the Wednesday night before the wedding to Tara, remember when you told me to stick to my own kind. I should have listened, because this bimbo retard here is abso-fucking-lutely clueless it seems." She barked pulling at her dress.

"I was angry and upset, I saw you with another bloke and told you to live your life," I explained feebly. "I got drunk and I don't even know who she is let alone remember it."

"So, how did Natasha Mason get hold of them?" she demanded.

"She told me the girl is her cousin, it was a set-up, apparently."

"You silver spoon lot, you're all bloody crazy, you know that." She barked and left the office. I followed her. "Screwing around, snorting cocaine, drinking champagne like its soda water and evidentially taking pictures of it."

"I have never snorted cocaine," I protested. "I tried pot and maybe a pill or two, but never the hard stuff."

"Oh, forgive me, I didn't realise that I was in the presence of a saint, St. Bullshit." She snapped.

"I have never professed to be a saint, Kelsey. You put me on the pedal stool, no one else." I retorted.

"Yes, well, I should have listened to myself then, when something seems too good to be true, it usually is."

"Yes, you should listen to yourself," I barked, "because you spend too much time listening to everyone else and all you really need to do is listen to your heart. This is Natasha's plan. You know what I have been through and what I didn't do, but still you are so ruddy quick to believe wrong of me. You don't trust me and if there is no trust then…"

"Go on." She goaded.

I didn't want to say it, she had backed me into that corner again, "Then there is no point to us, is there?"

"And here it is. You lied and you accuse me of not trusting you, you lied to my face and on the phone about where you have been, who you have been with and who you are fucking. Then when I challenge you, you blame me." She roared.

"I have never blamed you, I wouldn't, this is all me. I warned you in the beginning what I was like. That I had a past and you were fine with it. Now, after two and a half years of marriage, now you have doubts about my love for you."

She stared for a moment, not blinking, just allowing the tears to run, my heart was crippling me with every agonising beat. "Who were they?" she asked sitting at the table.

I sat opposite her, "I don't remember them because they don't matter, they never mattered."

"You said nothing matters," she accused.

"That's when all of this crap was going on. Look, I fucked up, okay? Is that what you want me to say? Me, I made a mistake and I allowed a psycho, control freak to call the shots for a little while. It's my fault, Kelsey, not yours, never yours. I don't blame you for this, I don't. I expected it and this is why I chickened out of telling the truth, I was afraid of admitting to you that I made a mistake and I was afraid of losing you. Especially after things were getting better between us," I admitted. She sniffed and wiped her cheeks of mascara soaked tears. "We went from kids falling in love, to a husband and wife and parents in a matter of months. I am not saying we were wrong or anything like that. I want this, I want this more than anything, I am just trying to help you see that this was never going to be easy for us. You say I don't tell you anything, this is why, because I know you will judge me and I have had that my entire life with my father."

"I don't mean to," she mumbled.

"I know, it's because you feel like you don't deserve to be happy, that there are no happy ever afters, to you they don't exist. But know this, you are my forever, Kelsey, you always will be." I reached towards her hands and she pulled them back.

"I'm sorry, Jeremy, but I can't do this right now."

"We need to talk about this." I reasoned.

"Yes, but I think you should go back to the party, I just need some time…"

"Time for what?" I frowned, my heart pounded painfully in my chest, throbbing in my emotionally strained throat.

"To think, I need time to think about everything, I have Harrison to consider."

"And I don't? He's my son too." I spat annoyed by her comment.

"I know, I would just prefer it if you left for a few days and gave me some breathing space." She stood from the table, "Please, just uh, just go."

"So, you're kicking me out," I sighed and stood also. "Thanks for understanding, Kelsey." I barked. "I'll go and pack some clothes then, if it's alright with you."

"Please understand how I feel." She frowned.

"I do, I understand that you would rather let a bunny boiler ruin our relationship than put up a fight for it." I retorted and left her in the kitchen.

I hurried up to our room and more or less threw my clothes into a case. I grabbed my shaving stuff and tooth brush from the bathroom, shut the case and carried it down stairs. She was hovering in the hall when I got there,

"Give a kiss to Harrison for me, I'll be at my father's if you need anything." I said and lifted my keys.

"What?"

"I said I am going to my father's."

"Why Canterbury, why go there?" she panicked.

"I have nowhere else to go," I replied candidly. "I can't stay at the Manor, my aunt and uncle are in Dubai and the place is being renovated after this weekend. Jude and Seb live in my old flat so there is nowhere else I can go. I will not live in my car."

"I don't want you to go all the way to Kent, what if Harrison needs you?" she said walking towards me.

"I'll be four hours away, that's all." I replied softly. She stared again, her mind was racing and her eyes looked so sore from crying. I was doing this to her and it cut me in two to think of the pain I was putting her through. "It's okay, I'll be alright." I assured her and turned to the door.

"Wait," she called out and ran towards me. "I don't want you to go, please, don't go." She began sobbing.

"Do you want me to stay?" I asked.

"I don't know," she cried. "I don't know what to do."

"I'm sorry, love, I just don't know what to tell you to make this right." I croaked, my own eyes filling with tears. My heart shredding as I watched her fall apart, piece by piece, my beautiful wife had come undone.

Nineteen

Kelsey

As angry as I felt, I couldn't watch him leave me, I just couldn't. I sobbed my heart out, sobbed until I had no tears left to cry. This was killing me, I wanted to thump him for being so stupid, but at the same time, I wanted him to hold me in arms and promise nothing like this would happen to us again. Yet my anger fuelled my stubborn streak and fear prevented me from letting him go.

"What do you want?" he asked.

"I don't know," I complained. Leaving the party as upset as I felt was not the best thing I had ever done. I could have crashed my car and I probably wouldn't have noticed. Those pictures, those filthy pictures of my husband with another woman, they were embedded into my brain, what the hell could I do? Let him leave me, no, no way. That was not an option, but I was so confused, angry and confused. "I need the toilet," I frowned and hurried into the downstairs loo, locking the door behind me.

I felt stupid and pathetic, weak and useless. I felt worthless and that Natasha had done this to me, she was destroying our marriage, was I prepared to let her win? Could I ever trust him again? I just didn't know what to do.

A gentle knock on the door disturbed my sobs, I sat on the floor by the door, "Kelsey, are you alright?" he asked.

"No," I answered truthfully. I think he slid down the door, it certainly sounded like he was just sat the other side of it.

"Did I ever tell you about the time I met my soul mate?" he asked.

"No," I sniffed.

"I was at a party in North Dorset. Life had been pretty shit if I am honest and I came south to spend a few weeks away from it all. My cousin suggested we throw a party in the hopes of cheering me up. I had been upset after catching my then girlfriend in bed with one of my best mates. Then to add insult to injury, she blamed me, so we argued for over an hour on the phone. I was outside in the gazebo fighting with her and when I turned around, I saw her, the most incredible looking girl I had ever seen." I smiled, I could see him in a light blue shirt, sleeves folded neatly up to his elbows and staring at me from the lit gazebo. "She had beautiful, long, blonde hair and wore a cream shirt. She looked sensational and something inside sort of flipped over. I told my ex it was over and switched off my phone, because from that moment on, I knew I had found her, my other half, my yang, my soul mate."

I smiled through my tears, they had stopped falling leaving my face sticky as they began to dry, "Go on," I said.

"I hurried inside to be found by Seb, *"I have this cracking bird you should meet,"* he told me. I wasn't interested in meeting anyone but the angel I had seen through the window. Luck has it, we Buxton's tend to think alike and he bought me to her, sat, perched on the end of the couch sat this amazing girl. *"This is Kelsey, from Bournemouth,"* he announced. I shook her hand and my heart leapt into life. Her huge blue eyes, eyes I could gaze at all day long, her glossy lips, just screaming at me to taste them. Her insatiable smile, everything about her amazed me and I wanted to know everything about her, but me being the plank I was I managed to upset her and she left." He paused for a few moments.

"Seb had arranged for us all to go to the beach and just the thought that I was going to see her again kept me awake for most of the night. I wanted to know everything about her and if it wasn't for the fact that her friend was busy in the summer house with Seb all night, I would have grilled her for every bit of information I could.

"I got up at the crack of dawn, showered and shaved. I wanted to look good for her, the concept of seeing her again excited and petrified me. She heard of my intolerance and made a salad for lunch, she was so thoughtful. I was captivated by her and had already fallen for her. I tried very hard to impress her and it only made me look a fool. She allowed me to rub sun tanning lotion over her insanely hot body and I needed a cool swim to save myself some embarrassment, I don't mind admitting that. I asked too many questions and it upset her resulting in her storming away from me at the beach. I found her at the beach cafe, she had calmed down somewhat and we had a coffee together. I could see she had been hurt, anyone could see that. But it didn't stop me trying.

"After calling a truce and her agreeing to me taking her to dinner, she stood on a weaver fish and I had to carry her from the beach back to the same cafe. I don't mind admitting that at the time, I would have carried her all the way home if she needed it. Her arms around my neck and her skin so close to mine, it felt like heaven. We ordained our relationship over a cup of pee and it saved her foot from almost certain amputation had I not saved her." I grinned, it wasn't that drastic, but it was nice that he remembered the details. "We had our dinner date that night which ended with a walk on the beach and our first kiss. I knew that this was the girl I wanted to spend the rest of my life with, she made me smile and she made me feel so alive."

"It turned out that I was to be her first lover, and that only made me want to be with her more. Not because it was some sort of conquest, but because I wanted to be *that* special person for her, the one she had saved herself for. Our first time made me feel like it was my first time too. I'd slept with too many girls, but none of them made me feel like my soul was merging with theirs, she certainly had something different. Not only a huge heart, a natural caring nature and an infallible love for me, she also made me want to be a better man, and that was pretty special.

"We're not perfect by any means, she is hot headed, like me, stubborn, like me. She feels she is not worthy of being loved, which is not true and she doesn't realise just how amazing she really is. The road hasn't always been smooth and we have hit many bumps, but one thing has remained and that's my unquenchable, irrefutable love for her. The more she gives me, the more I want. She is my perfect piece of heaven and I know that when two halves of a soul merges together the way ours has, well, that is something worth fighting for." I sniffed and placed my hand against the door. If I meant so much to him, then why was I always the one being hurt and lied to? "Kelsey, please, open the door." I could hear anger begin to writhe in his voice, something hit the door and I jumped back. "Open it now," he roared. "I will kick this door in," he snarled.

"Stand back," I ordered. "I won't open it if you are going to shout."

"Fine," he snapped. I opened the door, he was leaning against the wall. "Do you want me to go?" he asked.

"No," I replied. Relief filled his face.

"What can I do to make this right?"

"I don't know, I don't want her to win though, I don't want her to think she succeeded." I answered.

"Okay, do you mind if I get a drink?"

"It's your house too," I shrugged. I must have looked a mess, I felt it.

"Well, it may be my house, but it certainly doesn't feel like my home right now," he sighed and left me in the hall.

I followed him to the kitchen and watched as he poured a glass of juice, "I'm sorry, Jeremy, but this is all too much for me to handle. I just can't get over the fact that some psycho is out to split us up, she also had you arrested and then I get seven messages from her, mostly pictures of you with other women, how do you want me to react?"

"I don't know, maybe you should ask yourself why you are so ready to believe her in the first place," he stated.

"I suppose it's just as you've said, I don't think I deserve you. Look how much we have already been through, losing a baby, splitting up, you sleeping with someone else, now this… it feels like there is a reason we shouldn't be together."

"If you say it's because we run in different circles, then I will lose it," he warned. "I love you, isn't that enough? I chose you over my family, my friends, my social circle. I chose you because I love you. I don't care about money or flashy cars, or who's holidaying where and who is wearing who. I did that and I hated it. I found you, the love of my life and even though sometimes you make me want to scream, I put up with it because, and I will say it again, I LOVE YOU!" His voice echoed in the empty house. I just stared, I don't know if I was shocked or what, but I had never seen him like this. "You know what, I wish I had shagged her now, not because I wanted to, but at least I would deserve this shit." He frowned and sat at the table. I stood shaking from head to toe, the pain this was causing inside was immense and I felt so sick again. "I'm sorry, I didn't mean that," he muttered. I sat opposite him and rested my hands on the table, clasping the together to hide their quivering.

"She is beautiful," I sighed.

"You are more beautiful."

"She is sexy too." I added.

"You are the sexiest woman I have ever known," he declared.

"But she can give you anything you want."

"I already have *everything* I want and that is this, you, Harrison and our home. I couldn't ask for more." He reached over the table and took my hands into his, rubbing his warm thumbs over my knuckles. "You are my moon, my stars and my galaxy. You are my world, my soul mate and my best friend. All I have ever wanted was to be loved as much as I love someone and that someone is you, my beautiful, sexy minx. You are my sunshine on a rainy day and my reason for living."

I looked up and gazed into his watery eyes, "Honestly?"

"Honestly," he nodded. His phone rang in his pocket and for one second I wondered if it was her. "Hello?" he frowned letting my hands go so that he could answer the phone, "Uh, yes, that's um, that's fine. No, not at all. I'll see you then." He ended the call and frowned at me again. "You thought that was her, didn't you?" he accused.

"No," I lied, of course I did.

"You are never going to be able to trust me again." He stood, the chair screeched on the floor as it slid back. "I'll go, Kelsey, you can't stand the sight of me. I'll find a hotel somewhere for the night. You have a lot of thinking to do." He walked to the door. "That was DCI Hollins, by the way, he is coming over for a statement at ten in the morning because I am pressing charges against Natasha."

"What?" I asked as my eyes welled with tears again.

"I am pressing charges against her. She deserves everything that's coming to her. I'll see you in the morning." He left the kitchen so I stood and chased after him; he lifted his case and headed for the front door.

"Jeremy, wait," I sniffed. He stopped and turned to me, "I will trust you, I swear I will, I just need to learn how to again."

"And I'll wait until you do," he muttered.

"Don't go," I cried.

"You look at me with such disgust. I can't stand to see the disappointment in your eyes." He shook his head.

"I am only disappointed in myself," I sobbed. "Can't you see that? I feel I failed you. I should have been a better wife and I should trust that you would never do anything to hurt me, but…"

"You are an incredible wife, but you don't trust me and that's not right, love."

"Please," I begged. "Don't go."

"It's better this way," he said and opened the door. "I'll see you in the morning." He closed the door and my heart exploded.

My legs collapsed under me as fell to the floor and sobbed, praying for this to be a nightmare, that I would wake up from it and he would be there smiling. I tried to get up, but my body felt so weak, as if my life had been drained from me. I was angry at him, he had hurt me, but I never wanted him to leave, not really. The pain radiated through my body as the realisation that we may be coming to the end of our journey hit home. What the hell was I going to do?

No, no, this was not happening, I had to find him, I had to make him come home. I wanted him home. He was my husband and we belonged together. I used the little strength I had to push myself up from the floor and put on my coat. I wiped my face with a tissue I found in my pocket, lifted my car keys and headed for the door. I pulled it open, Jeremy turned around, he was crying, tears streamed his face and I hadn't seen that since his mother had died.

"I can't do it," he sniffed. "I can't go, I can't leave you." Relieved and determined, I dived at his body and threw myself into his arms. He was mine, mine and no up-tight, spoiled socialite was going to stake a claim on my husband ever again. "I'm sorry, sweetheart, I am so sorry." He cried into my hair.

"I'm sorry too," I admitted and I was, I felt it the second he had closed the door, sorry for everything I had done and not done. "I love you, okay? We will get through this, together." I asserted. He nodded and pressed his tear soaked lips against mine. Taking his hand in mine I led him inside and locked the door. "Let's go to bed," I told him.

I led him up to our room where he stripped me to my underwear before stripping himself. I climbed onto the bed and turned to face him. Pushing his fingers up the outside of my legs drove me wild. His fingers hooked under my knickers and he pulled them down my legs and over my ankles, tossing them over his shoulder.

I grabbed at his hair and pulled him towards my mouth, twenty four hours I had been left since his sensual massage and all I wanted was to feel him inside of me again. But no, Jeremy had other plans first.

Starting at my ankles, he trail soft kisses up my legs, while smoothing his hand where his lips had left a cool trail. When he reached my pelvis, he kissed me just below my belly, making me wriggle where it tickled so much. Soon his fingers found me, throbbing and wet, pulsing with my heart, but I didn't want to come like this, I wanted it to be when he was inside of me, I wanted him to blow my mind the way he had already with his words, talk about talking your way into someone's underwear, it had certainly done the trick on me.

"I want you," I moaned pulling his hand away from me, "I want you now."

He gazed into my eyes, "Calm down," he told me gently, I frowned, "we have all night." He added and smiled.

"Screw that, get on with it," I grinned and pulled him towards me.

As he pushed inside of me, I moaned with sheer pleasure. I locked my legs at my ankles, causing him to push in further; he kissed me before he began to move within me, thrusting deeply and slowly. I began to move with him, like liquid silk moulding together, we moved in perfect rhythm and harmony, we became one.

I dragged my nails up his back and he groaned out in pain. "Shit love," he said breathlessly, "that hurt."

"Just helping you to remember, you belong to me, that you're mine."

He grinned, his eyes dancing with desire as we rocked together, his thrusts deepening with every pulsing throb. "Yes...I...am!"

Waves of ecstasy washed over me as we reached the cusp of orgasmic bliss together, slowly coming down like two feathers floating on the breeze, we slowed our rhythm and he licked his dry lips.

He gazed into my eyes, "I love you so much," he said sincerely.

"I love you too," I smiled. That I already knew, what I didn't know was, if I would ever believe him when he left me to go out somewhere again and that scared the living daylights out of me.

Twenty

Jeremy

Frozen to the front doorstep, I stood there with my case in one hand and my keys in the other, I couldn't move a muscle. I couldn't leave her and why? Because I loved her, I loved her too much and she had to know. I thought about how I could tell her, tell her that my heart was shredding, that it felt like I was being torn apart. She had to know, I owed her that, just like I owed her the time she needed to build that trust in me up again.

I had lied to her, over and over again, I had lied and she had every right not to trust me. But I couldn't stare at those accusing eyes, so full of bewilderment and pain and what hurt more was knowing that I had done that to her.

Her sobbing had stopped and I thanked God, because it made me feel sick to hear what I was doing to her, she did not deserve this shit, she didn't. She hadn't done anything wrong, she was my perfect wife, so how had I managed to turn this around and put this on her shoulders? Because that's what pathetic arseholes that lie to their wives do. They manipulate them into thinking this is their fault, they turn it around on them and let them doubt their feelings and I could have just got into my car and left her, but I didn't, because I knew this was my fault and my doing, not hers.

I didn't know that I had tears streaming my face until I turned around and the cool October wind blew across my soaked face. She frowned, but I could see she was relieved to see me there.

"I can't go," I admitted, "I can't leave you." She dived into my arms and more tears flooded from my eyes as relief filtered through my body, "I am so sorry, sweetheart," I cried into her hair. She kissed me and led me inside.

Fuelled by emotion alone, I seduced my beautiful wife, teasing her body until she quaked on the verge of orgasm. When I finally placed myself inside of her, she dragged her nails up my back and it bloody hurt.

"Just helping you to remember, you belong to me, that you're mine." She told me, I could only agree and decided to never let anyone or anything threaten our marriage again.

As our bodies slowed, our pulses calmed and our heartbeats calmed, I held her in my arms, her body draped over the side of mine where she drew circles on my chest with her finger nails.

"Are you alright?" I asked her.

"Yes," she replied, but she didn't sound sure.

"But?"

"Where would you have gone tonight? If I hadn't have come out to you, I mean."

"Probably back to the party, but more than likely nowhere. I think I wouldn't have been able to drive away." I frowned. "I never want to leave you, sweetheart, it literally tore my heart to shreds realizing that we could lose everything we had fought so hard for." She squeezed a little tighter and I pressed my lips against the top of her head. I felt water drip from her face, "Kelsey?" I frowned. She looked up to me. "What is it?"

"I'm scared," she sniffed as more tears fell, "I am scared that I will lose you and never love or be loved like this again."

"Oh, darling, I am never going to leave you, not even in death. I will be with you forever. This I swear to you. No one has ever meant as much to me and no one ever will." I caught her tears on my finger, "I am not going anywhere." I promised. She nodded and kissed me, her salty tears seeped through our lips and tingled on my tongue. As we parted she gazed into my eyes.

"I love you so much," she said.

"And I love you too," I declared.

I held her all night, I heard Stuart return and go to his room and then I laid there thanking God for giving me another chance with my wife. I couldn't sleep, I had too much running around in my head. The prospect of losing my job was nothing in comparison to losing my family, but I fought for that and I knew I could fight just as hard for my job if I had to.

Having Natasha charged with harassment wouldn't do much except send a clear message to her that I wanted nothing more to do with her and to Kelsey, showing that I didn't feel sorry for her, Natasha deserved everything she had coming to her, I know I keep saying it, but she did.

I got up early and took a shower, shaved and dressed before going down to the kitchen to make a pot of tea. Kelsey slept soundly as she had for most of the night, she didn't even stir as I climbed out of bed. The hot water in the shower stung my back, her territory markings made me smile, she felt the need to show I was hers and that felt awesome.

I took her up a cup of tea and placed it on the bedside cabinet, I sat beside her and pressed my lips to her bare shoulder peeping out from under the quilt. She breathed in deeply and smiled before opening her eyes.

"Morning," I smiled.

"Good morning," she replied.

"I have made you tea and I am going to call your mother to check on Harry, so you take a shower or a bath, there is no rush, okay?"

"I could get used to this, Mr Buxton," she said stretching her arms out, allowing the quilt to fall away from her breasts. I stroked my index finger down the side of her soft skin and grinned at her nipples as they hardened. Her cheeks blushed slightly, I leaned in and kissed her, cupping her breast in my hand. She grabbed at the back of my hair and held my mouth against hers, "If you keep that up, you won't be going anywhere." She said, her mouth still pressed to mine.

I smiled, "Mmm, sounds wonderful, but we are not alone, Stuart came in just after three so…"

"Oh," she let me go and pulled the covers over her body, "we'll wait until later then."

"I just might hold you to that," I winked and stood from the bed. "Are you hungry?"

"Not for food," she smiled warmly.

"You can be such a tease," I chuckled. "Don't ever change that." I added and left her in bed.

Harry had been an angel and I asked if they minded keeping him there while I made my statement to the police. Jane agreed that it would be better to keep him there. I promised we'd pick him up as soon as we'd finished with DCI Hollins. He was now due around ten, he had called during my argument with Kelsey to explain that he'd need to come earlier. Of course she thought it was Natasha, if it was the other way around, I would think exactly the same.

When Kelsey came down a good half of an hour or so later, she was wearing a black dress and her knee length boots, her hair was pinned up and she looked sensational, seriously, I pictured laying her on the table and having crazy, passionate sex with her there and then, she looked so hot.

"I have to go out this morning, you don't need me here, do you?" she asked.

"Why do you have to go out?" I asked frowning, I would have liked to have had her there for support.

"I promised to help Jude, a wedding thing." She replied despondently.

"Oh," I frowned. She seemed a little off and extremely vague. "Are you alright?" I asked her.

"Yes," she replied and poured herself another cup of tea. As she turned, her face told me a different story.

"Kelsey?" I frowned.

"Good morning, Buxtons," Stuart announced as he waltzed into the kitchen, wearing his blue striped robe and Spiderman PJ bottoms, his hair was a mess, but he looked happy, "I hope all is well."

"Of course it is," Kelsey answered and sipped her tea. "Why are you in such a good mood?"

"I don't know," he shrugged.

"Is it to do with a certain young intern?" she smiled.

"Maybe," he grinned, "my lips are sealed."

She sipped her tea again before putting the cup on the table, "I won't be long," she added and lifted her bag.

"It's Sunday," Stuart frowned, "where are you going?"

"I have to see Jude," she said. "I'll see you later." She then left the kitchen.

"Kelsey," I called out chasing after her, "what's going on?"

She turned to face me, "I'll tell you later," she said and pecked my lips.

"I love you," I told her. She smiled wryly taking the collar of my shirt between her fingers and staring for a few moments.

"I love you too," she said and left.

I stared after her for a while, I don't know why, but I felt she was distracted by something and it was a little unsettling. I didn't have too long to ponder on it, DCI Hollins arrived dead on ten and we sat at the kitchen table while I made a statement about everything. I then printed off all of the emails she had sent me and forwarded all of the text messages to a number he had given me.

She was apparently out on bail after Dear Daddy came down from London and threw a fit until the judge agreed to release her. She was bailed to the Crown and under instructions that if she should try and contact me or come near me, she will be re-arrested and held in custody until she had to go to court. That made me feel so much better.

I signed the statement and DCI Hollins left after about an hour and a half. By this time, Elliot had arrived for his lunch date with Stuart and I needed to go and collect Harry from his grandparent's.

Before leaving the house I tried to call Kelsey, but her phone was switched off, so I tried Jude, I wasn't checking up on her, I merely wanted to make sure she was alright. Jude said she hadn't seen her at all and never even made plans to see her, which begged a few questions, where was my wife and why did she lie about where she was going?

Harry was so pleased to see me when I arrived at my in-law's house. He had been well looked after and smelled so good. I stayed for a cup of tea and explained about the statement I had made against Natasha in the hopes that not only will she leave me alone, but Kelsey knew that nothing she tried meant a thing to me. Jane assured me that Kelsey wouldn't think that I could cheat on her, of course she knew nothing of the night before and as tempted as I was to tell her, I felt it was something Kelsey would prefer we kept it between us.

We got home and I still hadn't heard anything from my wife. I was sick with worry, anything could have happened. She wasn't answering her phone, it just went straight to her voice mail. I pleaded with her to call home and let me know she was alright. I should never have let her go out alone, she had been through so much and anything could have happened, an accident, anything.

I gave Harry some lunch and decided to cook a meal for that evening, hoping it would take my mind off the fact that she could be missing. I made Spanish Chicken with my own sauce and put it in the oven on a low heat allowing the sweet, tomato and bell pepper aromas fill the house.

Shortly after three Kelsey's car pulled onto the drive, I jumped up from the couch and waited for her to come in. She had been crying, but she still looked in control.

"Where have you been?" I asked.

"Put the kettle on and I'll tell you everything." She stated.

Twenty-One

Kelsey

I had everything I wanted to say in my head, everything. I didn't want to tell Jeremy where I was going and who I was meeting and for the first time in a long time, I actually lied to him. While I showered that morning I received a message, threatening me and my husband, she dared to even try and contact me after everything she had done, I wanted to scratch her eyes out.

So far, Natasha hadn't met me or seen the impact of what she had tried to do to us, so I decided that it was time I let her threaten me to my face. She said she would ruin us, that her father's solicitor was already drawing up papers to sue us and I was not having that. She was not going to threaten us or do anything to us and I was going to be the one to tell her so.

I left quickly before I lost my nerve. I didn't like lying about Jude, but felt confident that once she found out what I was doing, she would understand. I drove to North Dorset in a blind fury, slightly apprehensive, but so determined to end this now.

I parked in the town car park and crossed the main road to the hotel. It was a fabulous looking building and it didn't surprise me to learn that she was staying here. The rooms were expensive and the food smelled delicious, but I would not allow it to intimidate me.

I could smell English breakfast as I entered the foyer and approached the counter. The young assistant manager, Shaun, who gave me Jeremy's phone smiled, "Good morning, how can I help you?"

"I would like to see Miss Natasha Mason please."

"Oh, uh, I am not sure if she is still in her room, she could be in the restaurant, I can..."

"No bother, she's expecting me," I lied, "I'll find her." I added.

"Uh, Miss...?" he frowned.

"It's fine, Shaun, thank you for being so helpful," I said over my shoulder and headed for the restaurant before he called security or tried to alert her, this had to be a surprise or it wouldn't work.

I weaved around the tables looking for her, I didn't really know what she looked like, I just imagined her to be stunning.

"Your Eggs Benedict, Miss Mason," a waiter announced behind me.

I turned on the spot and there she sat, at a small table for two, she set down the newspaper as the waiter placed her breakfast in front of her. I straightened my back and pulled shoulders up. I walked towards her table, my legs shook as I took in her perfectly conditioned hair and white tipped, manicured fingernails. She lifted her cup of coffee to her lips and sipped loudly as I took a deep breath and sat opposite her.

She set down her cup and stared, she recognised me instantly, a little colour flushed her cheeks as she gazed around quickly and wiped the sides of her full, red lips with a white, cotton napkin,

"Can I help you?" she asked tartly.

"I'm…"

"The little wife," she frowned.

"Yes, the little, stupid, bimbo wife, I believe you accused me of being." I retorted.

"Well, if the crown fits and all of that," she smirked.

"No, sweetheart, I don't need a crown when I already have everything I have ever wanted." I stated as I rested my hands on the table in front of me, allowing the sunlight to sparkle on my diamond engagement and wedding rings. She glanced down at them and frowned.

"So, Kelsey, how can I help you?"

"You can tell me why you thought it was okay to go after my husband." I answered.

"You need to know the truth."

"I do, I know that because you can't get your own husband, you are trying to take mine. I know that you can have anything you want, but the trouble with that is its boring, so you like to play games and try and ruin lives." I sat forward. "I also know why no man will ever freely get involved with someone like you."

She smiled, "Oh, do tell."

"You are high maintenance, like the celebs you write about, you get bored easily and no man has ever refused you before, getting everything you want is easy, but because Jeremy said no, it challenged you." I replied. "Trouble is, he loves me too much to ever forsake what we have for something so toxic, so poisonous as you."

"Of course he would tell you that…" she scoffed.

"Actually, I heard everything he told you, the discs with your meeting on them on Friday were played to me by Sebastian his cousin, you, my sweet, are looking at going to prison, you must be frightened."

"My father…"

"Has been sent a copy of the discs and all of the e-mails and messages you have sent us over the last few weeks. You see, I may only be a commoner, I may also be blonde, I don't live in a giant mansion and I don't have diamonds in my champagne, I have never needed that, all I have ever wanted was a loving, loyal husband and guess what, I have that. I am not the naïve girl you thought I was and you have just made the biggest mistake of your life." I leaned closer, "I have everything I need on you and I am going to make sure that every tabloid paper in the industry gets a copy of the discs and messages to show the world what you are like. I doubt you'll be able to show your ugly mug in London or Hollywood again."

"I will sue you for everything," she frowned and snarled through gritted teeth.

"I'd like to see you try. We have already met with a solicitor too and after Jeremy's statement this morning, the police will be able to charge you with everything from harassment to sexual assault and you will be finished. Your magazine sales will bottom out and there isn't a serious press in the world that will touch you by the time we have finished."

"You wouldn't," she frowned.

"I would and I will," I stated smugly.

"No one will believe you," she looked nervous.

"Oh they will, people believe anything and let's face it, that sort of mud sticks." She just stared, I honestly think she was at a loss for words. "So, if you don't want me to ruin your life you had better listen. You are going to accept your charges and wear any punishment they hand out to you and you are going to leave my husband and me alone. Anymore messages, threats and lies and I swear to God, Natasha, I will ruin your life the same way you have tried to ruin mine. You are also going to tell your father to back off suing The Press, Jeremy has done nothing wrong and should not lose his job because of you."

"Anything else?" she asked sourly.

"Yes, if you ever try to touch my husband again, I will smack those pearly whites down your throat. Yes, I am as common as muck and I don't give a flying fuck about my reputation. I fought my way through school and I have beaten off an ex. I actually have a black belt in Karate and I will kick your arse from here to Harley Street if you come near us again, understood?"

"Yes," she nodded.

"I mean it…" I snarled.

"I understand, I'll talk to my father." She promised. I stood from the table. "I, um, I am sorry." She frowned.

"You will be if you ever try to contact us again," I asserted and turned to leave.

"Kelsey, tell Jeremy I never meant for it to go this far."

"Why, so he'll take pity on you? Never. You did this, Natasha and you deserve everything that happens from now on. I just hope you learn from it." I stated and left.

I shook with both adrenaline and fear as I walked out of that restaurant and instead of going back to my car, I walked along the river for a while. I needed to calm down and I knew she could call the police and have me charged now, but after my threats I doubted she would.

I just needed some air and some time to think. After everything she had done, facing her like that took everything I had in me to keep it under control and I hoped this would be the end of it now. I actually pitied her as she had to sit there and listen to me and my threats, but I also felt I needed to say something to her. It's all a little guiltless fun until you have to come face to face with the innocent victim, then it changes and I hoped she got that message once and for all.

The warm autumn sun shone down on my hair in golden beams through the rust coloured tree branches. Winter was coming fast and with Harrison's hospital appointment the following day, I needed a clear head and mind to be able to face it. We'd had a good few weeks with him, though with everything that had gone on, I wondered if he felt neglected in anyway.

The crisp, dry leaves crunched under my boots as I made my way back to the car. The sun was low in the sky and I knew it was time to go home. As I climbed into my car it was almost twelve. Not quite ready to go home, I stopped at my Aunt Diane's in Winterborne Kingston.

As I climbed out of my car, I gazed at the house allowing all of the happy memories I had from the summer of rain with Jeremy fill my mind and lift my heavy heart. It reminded me of why I fell in love with him in the first place, we were perfect for each other and that was all that mattered. A commoner and a Diplomat's son, we had our flaws, our imperfections, but we fit, like two pieces of the same puzzle, we were connected and it started right there, in that small North Dorset village that didn't even have a shop, I met my soul mate and I fell in love.

We talked over tea and it made me realize that maybe we all needed a change, that maybe if we moved near to Blandford then Jeremy would be closer to his job, well, if he still had a job after the investigation. The prospect excited me and after another cup of tea, I hugged my Aunt Diane and Uncle Jeff goodbye and headed home.

When I arrived back I could see he was worried, his lips had lost their colour and looked dry. Harrison made a huge fuss over me and I held him in my arms for as long as you can actually hold a toddler who had a thousand better things to do than be cuddled by his mother.

The house smelled amazing, he didn't cook often, but when he did, he always filled the house with an amazing aroma that made my mouth water. He made some tea while I sat at the table, placing a cup in front of me before he sat down.

"I have been to see Natasha," I said.

"What?" he frowned, "Are you crazy?"

"I was going crazy, I wanted to talk to her, I wanted to know why she thought she could stake a claim on my family? I'd had more messages from her and I wanted them to stop," I replied.

"You don't know what she's like." He sighed shaking his head.

"I do now," I shrugged and sipped my tea.

I told him everything that was said, the threats and the promises made. I told him how she reacted and how I felt that the matter was now closed. He wasn't happy about it, but I didn't care. She had tried to burst our bubble and I was prepared to fight for us, Natasha had to know that.

"Do you think she'll back off?" he asked.

"I did threaten to beat her up if she didn't," I shrugged.

He smiled, "That is so sexy," he beamed, "did you tell her about your black belt?" he then asked reaching over the table and taking my hand.

"Yes, as a matter of fact, I did." I smiled.

"My wife, fighting for my honour, I have never heard of anything so sexy before," he said and lifted my hand to his lips.

"Most men would feel ashamed to allow their wife to fight for them," I frowned.

"Not this man, I can't think of anything more of a turn on." He admitted. "You still haven't taught me any moves."

"Well, maybe I should; I can't go around fighting all of your battles for you, they'll think I am your bodyguard, not your wife." I smiled.

"I don't care what they think, you are mine and that's all that matters to me."

"So, you are not mad at me for going to see her?"

"I am furious, it could have gone so wrong, it still can, but maybe she needed to face you, to know that you are not prepared to just sit back and let her get away with it." He stood and pulled me to my feet. Folding his arms around me he buried his face in my shoulder and inhaled deeply. "I love you so much, Mrs Buxton."

I smiled, "I love you too." He moved his head and met my lips, we kissed briefly and parted. "Now, I am starving, how long till dinner?"

"Not long, my lady." He grinned. "Kelsey, thank you."

"For what?"

"For believing me, for believing in us."

"I made my vows to you and they will last a lifetime." I declared.

After an amazing meal, we tucked Harrison into bed and shortly after, we went to bed ourselves, we were both exhausted. My head hit the pillow and not even Jeremy's soft kisses on my shoulders could keep me awake.

We arrived at Southampton General an hour before our appointment the following morning. I was so glad we went to bed early and all of us slept so well, the best I had slept in a long time. We liked to get there early for Harrison's appointments as we never knew if we would be able to park or not. We made our way to the children's ward and waited in a room for the doctor.

I almost fell over when a new doctor came in and smiled, "Martin?"

"Kelsey?" he grinned, "Oh, my God, you look sensational."

"So do you." I beamed. Jeremy fidgeted in his seat. "Oh, this is my husband, Jeremy and the little one destroying your Lego house is Harrison."

He held out his hand to Jeremy, "It's great to meet you."

"And you," Jeremy said, shaking his hand. "Oh, Martin, the doctor from Majorca." Jeremy nodded.

"That's right," Martin smiled, "I'm Doctor Martin Selby and I am Harrison's new heart specialist."

"How uncanny," I smiled.

Martin was wonderful with Harrison, he had gained a little weight since I last saw him, but I put that down to having a wife cooking for him, although I couldn't see a ring or anything, I knew he was determined to marry his fiancé. We chatted as he examined Harrison and suggested we take him for a scan.

"You can go in with him, but I have to ask, is there a chance you could be pregnant?" he looked at me and I looked at Jeremy.

"Um, I don't know," I frowned.

"Right, well, Jeremy, you'll have to come in then, because it is vital we have this scan today. I need to see if there are any changes in his heart since he was last scanned." I nodded and watched as they left.

In all honesty, I couldn't remember the last time I had a period. I had been so wrapped up in Harrison and then the Natasha crap, I hadn't really taken notice. While they were in having the scan, I went to see Tracey, one of Harrison's nurses.

She greeted me with a hug and when I told her my dilemma, she suggested doing a quick ultra sound to see if I was pregnant. Of course I didn't believe I was, but maybe all of the stress was taking its toll on my body and hoped that the tiredness and nausea I had felt of late was just stress and nothing else. But nothing could mistake that flicker on the screen, a clear image of a perfect heartbeat.

"You are pregnant," Tracey smiled.

"I can't be," I frowned.

"Have you had periods?"

"I can't remember the last one I had."

"Was it maybe four months ago? Because you, my love, are already sixteen weeks preggers and this one is due around April the eighteenth."

"Bugger," I frowned.

"Harrison is going to be a big brother," she beamed. "A spring baby, how wonderful."

"Yes, wonderful." I sighed and zipped up my jeans. She handed me a picture of the baby and hugged me again.

I didn't say anything to Martin or Jeremy; I felt I needed time to digest the information before announcing it to the world. It's weird, because as soon as she said I was, I felt pregnant, bloated and nauseated, terrific. Martin said they would have Harrison's results soon and promised to call us as soon as he had the information to tell us.

"So, Martin was nothing like I imagined." Jeremy admitted as we left the hospital.

"How did you imagine him?" I asked.

"I don't know, like he should be on TV or something," he shrugged. "Nice bloke though, bloody good doctor too. He was so good with Harry."

"He loves children," I smiled remembering the night I met him. "He told me he was going to specialize in paediatrics while we were in Majorca." I could see him frown, "I told you nothing happened, he was very nice and looked after me after the girls had abandoned me to dance the night away."

"A doctor and a gentleman, I am surprised he is not married."

"He is, isn't he?"

"No, apparently not," he answered. I didn't want to push the issue, not that it mattered, I was happily married and nothing could have changed my mind, not even the imminent patter of tiny feet that was about to grace our lives again.

The traffic wasn't as bad as I thought it would be for a Monday as we headed back to Poole. I had hidden the picture that would tell Jeremy the one thing he tried hard not to press me on, although I could see in his eyes that he was dying to find out if I felt pregnant and what I would do if I was.

"What if you are?" he finally asked as we hit the motorway.

"What if I am what?" I frowned pretending I didn't know what he meant.

"Pregnant?"

"Mmm, we'll talk about it when we get home." I muttered.

"Are you okay?"

"Yes, I'm fine," I stiffened, but I saw his eyes roll, he knew when something was up and it was an uncomfortable thirty mile trip home.

Jeremy put Harrison to bed while I made some tea, in my bag I had the picture of our new baby, but I didn't know if I should tell him yet. Didn't we have enough going on? He kept on though, pressing for a response, asking questions, I couldn't lie to him, not on this. I learned the hard way last time, I stood from the chair and walked to my bag, I pulled out the picture and handed it to him. He frowned and then he smiled, I mean, his face lit up like a Christmas tree,

"So, you are?"

"Yes," I nodded.

"That's, um, that's fantastic news," he smiled, his eyes filled with tears, "we're having another baby." He gushed wiping the tears from his eyes.

"It's due the eighteenth of April," I frowned. "Jeremy, can we do this, I mean, well, Harrison is so sick and…?"

"What's your point?" he asked looking up at me.

"Will we cope?"

"We'll have to cope. It's called life, Kelsey, it's a challenge but I am so happy, I want to scream it from the hills. We're having a baby." He leapt up and swept me up into his arms, "God, I love you, you have made me the happiest man alive."

"And you are sure you want this baby?" I checked.

"Of course I am sure," he said and pulled back gazing into my eyes. "A new baby, Kelsey, we'll be a family of four."

"I won't be able to be Jude's bridesmaid in April now," I explained.

"She'll understand," he grinned. "I am going to call home." He kissed me and left me in the kitchen. Bewildered and I suppose in shock.

I sat back on the chair and placed my hand on my tummy. It hadn't swelled at all, four months already and I hadn't a clue. As I panicked over coping with a sick toddler and a new born baby, I felt a little flutter inside, it made me smile, as if the baby was telling me that we would be fine and I thought that maybe we would be.

Twenty-Two

Jeremy

Trying to hold Harrison still so that they could scan him was like trying to hold an octopus still under water. He wriggled and cried and moaned and screamed, but Martin needed the scan so it had to be done. The whole time though I kept thinking about Kelsey and wondering if she was pregnant. It would explain a lot, her emotions were all over the place, she slept really well at night and she had a glow about her, an insatiable glow. But then I remembered all of the shit I had put her through of late and all of those symptoms could also be stress.

She seemed a little distracted during the drive home and I felt like a cat on a hot, tin roof, I was excited to find out. We'd been so wrapped up in Harrison and Natasha bullshit that it hadn't occurred to me that we'd used no contraceptive for months. She was meant to be taking the pill, because she forgot to take it regularly, we were back to using condoms, but we hadn't in ages. She could be pregnant and this time I could be there from day one, I could do it right this time.

I put Harrison to bed for his afternoon nap and hurried down to see her. Something was on her mind. She had made tea and I wanted to know if we should do a test.

"Shall I go to the Pharmacy and get you a testing kit?" I asked.

"No," she shook her head.

"Don't you want to know?" I pressed. "I know I do."

"What difference will it make?" she sighed and sipped her tea.

"Well, it would make a lot of difference. We'd need to plan things out, decorate the spare room. I'd certainly have to think about a new job if I lose this one." I replied. She just stared and stood from her chair. She reached into her bag and pulled a piece of paper out of the inside pocket.

"Here," she frowned and handed it to me.

I turned it over. It was an ultra sound picture of a baby, our baby. "So, you are?" I checked.

"Yes," she nodded.

I felt my face glow as my eyes filled with tears blurring the image, "That's fantastic news, Kelsey. We are having another baby." I wiped my tears so I could see it clearly.

She didn't appear to share my elation, "It's due the eighteenth of April." She sighed, "Jeremy, can we do this, I mean, well, Harrison is so sick and...?"

"What's your point?" I asked impatiently.

"Will we cope?" she asked.

"We'll have to cope. It's called life, Kelsey," I replied. "It's a challenge, but I am so happy, I want to scream it from the hills. We're having a baby." I stood and swept her up into my arms, "God, I love you, you have made me the happiest man alive." I declared.

"And you are sure you want this baby?"

"Of course I am sure," I said in certainty as I pulled back from her gazing into her amazing blue eyes. "A new baby, Kelsey, we'll be a family of four."

"I won't be able to be Jude's bridesmaid in April now," she explained.

"She'll understand," I shrugged, "I am going to call home." I pecked her lips and hurried out to the phone. I had a feeling she didn't really want this baby and selfishly thought that the more people I told, she'd have no choice but to continue the pregnancy. It hit me hard as I went to lift the receiver, was she okay?

I returned to her without making a call, I wanted to make sure she was alright with expecting again. I knew how much Harrison put her through and I was well aware of the fact that he was extremely sick. But I also thought that maybe this was what we needed, a bigger stamp on the world. What better way to tell the likes of Natasha Mason that I loved my wife and that she loved me than having another baby?

She was sat on the couch with her hand pressed across her tummy, tears streamed her face,

"Sweetheart," I panicked and ruched to her side. "What is it?"

"Nothing," she sniffed and brushed her tears aside with a quivering hand. "I'm a little overwhelmed, that's all."

"You asked me if I am happy about this and I told you I am, but I didn't ask you. Are you happy?"

She stared as I sat beside her, "I am shocked and I didn't know if this was what I wanted right now at this point in time..."

"But?"

"I think I just felt my first kick and it made me realise that no matter who tries to get between us, who tries to ruin what we have, we always come out stronger on the other side. This baby is fighting against the odds, the stress and all the shit we have been through these past weeks, this baby is telling me that we can do anything together." She explained. "Timing couldn't be worse, but something is working hard to make sure we have more reasons to stay together, I can't argue with the forces." She smiled.

"So, can I call my sisters and tell them?" I asked.

"Of course you can, we're already sixteen weeks, so as far as I am concerned, we're in the safe zone."

"Did I tell you how much I love you today?" I asked with a smile of delight.

"Yes," she grinned, "but I'll never get tired of hearing it."

"I love you to the moon and back."

"Only the moon?" she checked.

"Well, I am a bit tired to today," I grinned, "I'll love you to infinity tomorrow." I kissed her and felt her smile beneath my lips.

"You had better," she said while still kissing me. I moved from her mouth and pressed my lips against her tummy, she was having my baby and nothing could ruin that day.

Hermione and Elle were ecstatic to learn that they were going to be aunties again. They more or less screamed down the phone and both invited themselves to ours for Christmas, how could I say no? Julian was still playing up, he had been caught with drugs on campus and faced being expelled from school on his first day back, the kid was acting like a plank. After the pot incident our father had threatened that if he continued to behave this way, he would send for him to join him in Austria. Part of me wanted him to send for Julian, after all, he obviously needed his father, but a huge part of me wished I was there for him. He also needed his big brother and I felt awful for allowing it to get so out of hand.

At dinner that night I told Kelsey about Julian and how worried I was about him,

"Has he asked for your help?" she asked.

"No, but..."

"Jeremy, if you go up there, or get him down here, he'll see it that you are interfering, he is nineteen, he needs to start to take responsibility for his actions. If he needs your help, I am sure he'll ask for it." She stated. She was right, but it didn't help me feel any better. "Your dad shouldn't have gone away so soon after your mother's death, Julian needed him."

"What if he gets kicked out of school?"

"He'll have to get a job." She shrugged. "He's a man, love, not a boy."

I nodded and sighed, "You're right."

"If he wants to come here, I would never turn him away, but he has to come here because it's what he wants."

I reached over and took her hand, "I am so lucky to have you."

"Don't ever forget it," she smiled.

We were in bed early, we were both exhausted but it didn't stop me making love to her. I slept in her arms with her warm, naked body was pressed against mine. For the first time in a long time, I actually prayed and thanked God for keeping us together, for allowing Kelsey to give us another chance and for giving us another baby. I fell asleep wondering if we would have another son or if we would have a daughter, the excitement burned in my tummy, boy or girl, I would be happy.

Two days later I sat in the meeting room at The Press waiting for Mark and Brian to join me. I had been summoned to the office after learning that Natasha had now been charged with sexual assault and blackmail. Mr Mason was out for my blood, even after Mark had showed him all of the messages, he refused to believe she was not his innocent little girl.

I had no idea that he was going to join us and as they entered the room, I jumped to my feet. My eyes fell on the short balding man dressed in a light grey suit with a sliver tie and highly polished black shoes.

"Jeremy, this is Mr Mason." Mark announced.

"Mr Mason," I acknowledged.

"So, you are the sneaky, little sod who is trying to ruin my daughter's life." He grumbled as he sat.

"Actually, your daughter has tried to ruin my life," I retorted.

"Well, that's not what she's told me." He shrugged.

"Really," I frowned and looked at Mark. "Because she would never lie, right?"

"Right," he affirmed.

"So, did she tell you how much she was paying The Press for the copy editing?" I asked.

"A hundred and fifty thousand per quarter," he answered.

"Sorry," Brian interrupted, "we have it on paper, it was meant to be a hundred grand."

"Natasha told me you wanted a hundred and fifty," he frowned.

"I can get the paperwork," Mark said. "Mr Mason, I don't think Natasha is as honest with you as you think she is. Jeremy is many things, he can be a jumped up twat some times, he has a short temper and can be a bit uptight, but he is not a liar. I believe him when he says he is innocent in this. Natasha tried to ruin his marriage and his job. Natasha has sent him obscene messages and sent them to his wife, a sweet girl who really doesn't deserve that."

"I have seen the messages." He sighed.

"The police have charged her, Mr Mason," I continued, "they have seen the video of our last meeting and how she admitted to it all."

He thought for a few moments, "I won't sue the company if you drop the sexual assault charges against her," he said glaring into my eyes. "I'll take her back to London, I'll send her to Hong Kong, but that one charge will ruin her life."

"But then I'll be admitting it didn't happen," I explained, "she touched me, sir and I have to ask, if I had done something like that to her, would you be asking for her to drop the charges?"

He shook his head, "No, I'd cut your bollocks off," he smirked slightly. "Fair enough, can't blame a father for trying, right?"

"Right," Brian agreed, "you can't blame a boss for having faith in his staff either. Jeremy, your job is safe with us, son."

Mr Mason stood, "Fine, its over then, I won't push this any further, but be rest assured, young man, if I ever find out that you did touch her, I'll come looking for you."

"I can arrange for a copy of the discs to be sent to you," Brian stated.

"You do that," Mr Mason groaned and left the room.

"So, when are you coming back?" Mark asked me.

I stood from the table and buttoned up my jacket, "I don't know if I want to come back," I said trying to keep a straight face, "You did just call me jumped up twat and that tells me that you don't respect me. I could never work for someone who doesn't respect me."

"Jez, you know I was only…"

"Tomorrow," I said. "I'll see you at eight in the morning."

"Excellent," Brian smiled. "I am sorry we put you through this."

"It's not been easy," I sighed.

Mark scoffed, "You are telling me, Seb has been trying to do your job, he knows as much about copy editing as I know about the female G-spot." He smiled. Brian burst into hysterics, "You know, because I am gay."

"I know," I smiled. "I am just amazed you actually know that there is a female G-spot." I snickered.

"Ha bloody ha," he laughed. "I'll see you in the A.M."

"You will," I nodded, "thank you, both."

"You are most welcome." Brian said and shook my hand.

I left the office feeling like I had a whole new lease on life. I had my job back, Natasha was out of my life forever and I was going to be a dad again. I only hoped that I never let Kelsey down again, the pain I put her through was immeasurable and still she came out fighting, fighting for us, for our family, fighting for me, how could I ever wrong her again? Plus the fact that she'd probably kick my arse if I did scared the life out of me. She was one tough cookie, there was no doubting the strength she had, a force to be reckoned with, my wife, my beautiful, pregnant wife.

Life had turned a dark and dismal corner that autumn and I plan to make the most of everything from now on. Yes, Harrison still needs an operation on his heart and we anxiously await the letter to tell us when that will be. Life is not perfect for us, yet, but for now, I'd take it. I'd take our little piece of heaven over the emptiness that could have quite easily replaced it any day.

The autumn had been tough on us both and I was actually glad to see the winter begin. The spring followed winter and that was one season I couldn't wait to embrace, a season of new beginnings and for us, a new life.

The End

About the Author

Melissa J Rutter lives on the south coast of England in the quay side town of Poole. She grew up nearby in the beach resort town of Bournemouth and after spending a year as a nanny in New Hampshire where she studied at the New Hampshire Institute of Art, she returned to her home and met her husband Francis. They have been happily married for fifteen years and have two wonderful children.

For more information on Melissa by visiting her website, MelissaJRutterAuthor.webs or by visiting her Facebook page, Author Melissa J Rutter. You can follow her on Twitter @MelissaJRutter. She is always happy to hear from her readers.

Other Novels:

Lunar Ryce, Soul Collector
Lunar Ryce, Soul Searcher
Lunar Ryce, Soul Savior
Diamonds to Dust
Back to Innocence
Summer Rain
Cruel Winter
Shadows Lost
Reflections Found
Lessons in Love
I, Immortal Book 1
I, Immortal Book 2, World in Flames
I, Immortal Book 3, Fire and Ice
Time To Breathe
Silver Bay Song
Same Difference

Coming in 2016
Lunar Ryce 4, Soul Redeemer
I, Immortal Book 4
Spring Fever.

36381369R00121

Printed in Poland
by Amazon Fulfillment
Poland Sp. z o.o., Wrocław